THE HOUSEMISTRESS

By

Keira Michelle Telford

www.venaticpress.com

www.venaticpress.com

SPECIAL THANKS

to

Mick Addleton
Anthony Boussetta

"What you call sin, I call the great spirit of love, which takes a thousand forms."

— Elisabeth von Bernburg, from the film *Mädchen in Uniform* (1931)

(adapted from the book *Das Mädchen Manuela*, written by Christa Winsloe)

CHAPTER ONE

LARKHILL BOARDING SCHOOL SMELLS LIKE plasticine. At least, the main foyer does. Sitting in an uncomfortable plastic chair outside the Headmistress's office, seventeen-year-old schoolgirl Rylie Harcourt taps the toes of her polished leather shoes against the tiled floor, wondering how much longer this is going to take.

Her parents are inside the office with the Headmistress, finalizing her admission, and she can hear every word they're saying about her. Why they bothered sending her out of the room in the first place is a complete mystery.

"We thought the discipline of a boarding school might be good for her," she hears her mother say with a heavy sigh. "It certainly can't hurt."

That's parent code for: We've tried everything, and we don't know what to do with her anymore, so now you can have a go.

It's par for the course as far as Rylie's concerned, and she hadn't been in the least bit surprised when the threat of boarding school was first mentioned. After all, they did the same thing to the family dog.

Wingles wouldn't stop humping the sofa cushions, so they sent him to a boarding and training facility called The Dog House. He was kept there until he started behaving in a more socially acceptable manner, then he was shipped back home, a reformed pooch.

Poor Wingles.

His spirit was irreparably crushed.

Sliding her hips forward in the chair, Rylie leans her head back and stares at the ornate ceiling. Plaster reliefs frame a large chandelier at the center, mimicking floral vines spreading outward and creeping down the walls. It all seems overly fancy just for the sake of being so, which is in keeping with pretty much everything else she's seen since her arrival forty minutes ago, starting with the large and totally pointless marble statue of the school's founder at the head of the driveway, the Larkhill motto inscribed on its base: Virtutem Et Musas.

Virtue and Learning.

The main school building itself is a sprawling Jacobean mansion with numerous additions added over the many decades since it became a privately run educational institution. This place is posh—as you'd expect for a private boarding school in Cambridge—and for Rylie's parents, that's even more important than the school's impressive exam scores and outstanding Ofsted inspection reports.

As time drones on, the *tête-à-tête* between her parents and the Headmistress continues, and the doublespeak abounds. When questioned as to why they felt the need for such an abrupt mid-term transfer instead of waiting for the new school term to begin, her parents reply simply: "She had some difficulty with a teacher."

Translation: She's disobedient, unruly, and insubordinate.

Upon being quizzed about their decision to enroll their only child in boarding school rather than moving her to another private day school, they say: "We thought the experience might be able to teach her a bit of responsibility."

Translation: We want her to grow up.

On their selection of Larkhill Boarding School in particular: "She needs a strict routine and some discipline."

Translation: We blame ourselves for her wayward behavior. We've indulged her far too much, and what she really needs is a good spanking.

Expounding on that: "She has fanciful ideas, shows no respect for the feelings of others, and needs to be given a healthy dose of reality."

Translation: She's displayed some lesbian tendencies, which we find deeply shameful, and she needs to be straightened out—in every sense.

Rylie's not quite sure how they think they're going to achieve that by sending her to an all-girls school, but she's definitely not complaining. She is sick of listening to them slander her, however, so she gets up and meanders around the foyer, killing time.

What started as a light drizzle an hour ago is now a downpour beating down outside. The full length glass doors at the main entrance offer an unbroken view of the school's lacrosse field to the right—large puddles already forming in the turf—and covered tennis, badminton, basketball, and volleyball courts to the left.

Catching her reflection in a mirror hanging on the wall beneath a large sign that reads 'Are you presentable?', Rylie ponders the pros and cons of her new uniform. The slip-on leather shoes are the same ones she wore at her old school—no change there. The knee high socks are almost identical, too, except these are black and her old ones were white. The pleated, plain black A-line skirt is a few inches longer than she'd like; it comes down to her knees. The white shirt is starchy and stiff, the top button undone; she feels like a rebel.

Her blue and gold tie hangs a little loose, which she'll probably get in trouble for, but she prefers it that way. Having something close against her neck makes her feel as though she's choking, and she hates that the tie is a compulsory part of the uniform. At least the colors are a vast improvement over her old school, which was a shade of orange so bright it almost fluoresced. It was the color of puréed carrots, but they called it tangerine. Either way, it was vile.

The worst part about this new uniform is undoubtedly the navy blue cardigan. When she first heard there was an option to wear a cardigan instead of a blazer, she thought that would be liberating. The blazer at her old school was heavy and thick, weighing her down and restricting her movement, but this cardigan does something far worse: it masks her boobs.

They're not that big to begin with, and now they're almost invisible. Perhaps that's the point of it, she thinks. The longer skirts, the flat shoes, and the potato sack cardigans are all designed to make the students look less sexually appealing to one another. Ugh. Now she's going to have to put more effort into her hair.

She drags her fingers from crown to tip, teasing out the tangles in her long, naturally blonde, wavy locks. Did she remember to brush it this morning? She hasn't the foggiest. To add insult to injury, makeup is strictly forbidden. She'd been permitted to keep on a subtle shade of pink lip gloss, but was forced to remove everything else. Never before has she felt so grateful for having a smooth complexion. Her only real complaint is that her pale blue eyes seem somewhat lost on her face without any mascara or eyeliner to make them stand out.

Bugger it.

She pivots away from the mirror, looking for something better to do than pick faults with herself, and a large notice board by the main doors is the first thing to draw her attention. It's chock-full of flyers for all sorts of different after-class clubs, but the sign-ups closed weeks ago. She'll have to wait until next term to start doing Pilates, or learn how to fly a kite like a champ, or take up wrestling, and the music group isn't going to be taking on any new members until after the summer.

Fortunately, things start to look better when she hears the clippety-clop of high heels and turns to see a woman skip up the steps to the front doors, sheltered from the rain by a large royal blue umbrella bearing the school crest. As she reaches the top of the steps, protected by the overhang of the building, she turns her back to the doors and shakes off her umbrella, trying to close it up without dropping a bundle of books she's carrying in her arms. At the same time, she backs into one of the glass doors, pushing on it with her bum, her cheeks pressed up against it, trying to open it without the use of her hands.

After a few seconds of watching her struggle, Rylie makes a move to help, but the brief hesitation costs her and someone else gets there first. The girl—uniformed, her hair matted from the rain, her clothes damp—runs up out of nowhere, her timing perfect. She takes the umbrella from the woman's hands, buttons it, then holds open the door.

"*Merci*," the woman purrs her thanks in French, checking the books to make sure she's managed to save them all from the onslaught of the weather.

The girl—about Rylie's age, her mousey-colored hair cut into a bob, her cheeks rosy from running to get out of the rain—hangs the umbrella on a rack near the doors, then returns to the woman's aid.

"Can I help you with anything else, Miss?" She holds her hands out to take the books.

"I don't think so, Edwards." The woman rejects the offer, her thick French accent making every word sound warm and sensual. "You're all wet."

That shouldn't sound dirty, but it does. The woman's positively oozing sexuality. Black stiletto heels accentuate long, stockinged legs, the hem of her pencil skirt a tasteful distance above her knees, her ass and hips hugged tightly by the formfitting fabric. Her cotton blouse is snug around the bust, the top four buttons left undone, creating a plunging neckline that reveals a splash of bare, milky skin, no jewelry to draw attention away from it.

13

Long hair in the deepest shade of brown is tied harshly back, neat bangs parted in the middle, not quite long enough to reach her eyebrows. As she brings a hand up to tuck a stray wisp of hair behind her ear, an amethyst cufflink catches the light. The shade of dark purple matches her earrings, which match the accenting in the frames of the reading glasses on her head, the arms tucked into her hair.

Sensing the attention of someone's eyes, she looks over and meets Rylie's gaze. Her lips are painted come-fuck-me red, slightly parted and curled into a small smile. Mascara-coated eyelashes flutter, her emerald eyes shimmering in the glare of the foyer lighting.

Rylie's not sure how much time passes this way, with blue eyes hooked unwaveringly on green, neither female able to break away, but it feels like hours.

"Are you new?" the woman asks at last, taking a step closer, turning her back on the other girl. "This is your first day?"

Rylie nods, clasping her hands behind her back so that she doesn't fidget. "Yes, Miss."

The woman keeps advancing, her stiletto heels clicking on the tiled floor. She has an elegant sway to her hips, the movement of her body hypnotic, her poise graceful and self-assured. When she gets within arm's reach, she extends a hand toward Rylie's face and fingers some hair out of her eyes, trailing a fingertip down her cheek as she moves the wayward lock of hair aside, lost in a reverie.

"You're very beautiful," she coos softly. "*Une très belle fille.*"

Over her shoulder, the wet girl is dripping onto the floor tiles, glowering. Rylie can see the look of disdain on the girl's face, but gives little regard to it. The gorgeous French woman is fawning over her—this is epic!

Much to her disappointment, though, the door to the Headmistress's office suddenly swings open, causing the woman to withdraw in a flash. Physical contact between a teacher and a student is, after all, meant to be explicitly prohibited.

"I must go." The French woman checks her watch, excusing herself immediately. "*Bienvenue à Larkhill!*" She welcomes Rylie to the school as she heads for the main staircase, calling over her shoulder to wish the newcomer good luck. "*Bonne chance!*"

Rylie is left feeling a little dazed. Did that really just happen? They didn't even exchange names. Who the hell was she? There's no time for contemplation. Her parents step into the foyer, followed by the Headmistress, Missus Bursnell, who sets on her without pause for any pleasantries.

"You'll have to brush that mop of hair and tie it back." She peers at Rylie's ears, examining her earrings. "Simple studs are permitted, but all other jewelry is forbidden." She examines one of Rylie's hands, picking at her black nail polish. "Clear nail lacquer only. You'll find polish remover in your dormitory bathroom." She drops the offending hand. "I'll fetch someone to give you a guided tour of the school, and that'll be all for today. You'll start classes as normal tomorrow morning." She hands over a thick pile of school supplies, naming them off one by one. "Year Twelve day planner, class schedule, book list, house rules—"

She goes on, but Rylie stops listening. Now in her late fifties, Missus Bursnell's probably been a teacher her whole adult life. At least, that's the impression Rylie gets. She has a practiced austerity about her, and a face that makes it appear as though she seldom smiles. Her lips are thin, slightly pursed, her cheeks somewhat gaunt. She has jowls, almost like a bulldog, as if all the plumpness from her face fell to her jawline when she hit menopause.

While one eye works actively to take in every detail of her surroundings—from the torrential rain outside, to the small puddle of water left behind where the scowling girl was standing before she practically chased the French woman up the staircase—the other eye remains eerily still. The two eyeballs aren't even the same color. One is paled from age and encroaching blindness, while the other is a rich hazel. The fact that it's a false eye couldn't possibly be any more shockingly apparent, even if it still had the price tag on it.

When she's done thrusting various things into Rylie's hands, including a key for her sixth form house, which she's told to guard like the Crown Jewels, Missus Bursnell pulls a cell phone from her pocket and taps out a quick message to one of the teachers in the building.

While waiting for the teacher to read the message and send forth the student who's been chosen to conduct the tour, Rylie's parents make a hasty departure, taking advantage of a temporary lull in the rainstorm. They tell her to behave, follow instructions, try to get along with everyone, and adhere to school rules—all the usual parent bullshit.

In the rush, they forget to say 'I love you', but that's not an uncommon oversight in the Harcourt household. Rylie stopped giving it too much thought a long time ago, and now's certainly not the moment to dwell on it. The doors are barely closed behind them when a bubbly girl with braided hair that's so blonde it's practically white runs down the staircase into the foyer, her rubber-soled shoes slapping against the tiles.

"No running!" Missus Bursnell barks before introducing them. "Set a proper example, for goodness sake." She shakes her head at the girl, tutting her disapproval. "Harcourt, this is Ellie Souliere, one of our Year Eleven girls. She's been a pupil here for almost five terms, and she'll be your tour guide this afternoon. It'll do her some good to practice her English with you."

As if being deliberately belligerent, Souliere ignores that last comment and holds her hand out to Rylie. "*Bonjour.*" She smiles warmly. "*Ça va?*"

"English, Souliere." Missus Bursnell sighs. "Don't be so stubborn." She shoos them both away. "Off you go now."

Grinning, Souliere grabs Rylie's hand and leads her away, excited to break with routine and spend the rest of the day leading the new girl around campus instead of being stuck inside a classroom doing algebra.

"What's your name?" She speaks slowly, pronouncing each word carefully.

"Rylie."

"Rye-lee," Souliere repeats to herself, thinking it over. "I like it very much," she concludes. "Which house have you been assigned to?"

Rylie consults one of the many sheets of paper in her bundle of supplies. "Carriveau."

"*Ah*! *Mademoiselle Vivienne Carriveau, la plus belle femme du monde*!" Souliere clasps a hand over her heart. "You have the most luck! She's the best Housemistress in the entire school. French, too," she adds with pride.

French? Rylie perks up at that. Could Carriveau be the woman she met in the foyer? The provocative, high-heeled brunette could certainly fit Souliere's enthusiastic and theatrical description: the most beautiful woman in the world.

"Are you in her house, too?" Rylie wonders, amused that Souliere is so besotted.

Souliere shakes her head. "Not yet had the chance." She points to an emblem on her blazer that identifies her as a Year Eleven pupil, en route to take her GCSE examinations in the coming summer. "*Je suis trop jeune*. That is, I am too young." She checks out a slightly different emblem on Rylie's cardigan. "You are Lower Sixth, *oui*? Year Twelve?"

Rylie nods. AS-level examinations will await her in the summer months.

"Sixth formers are housed separately," Souliere goes on to explain. "More freedoms and such. Like using an iron without supervision and doing your own laundry."

"And Miss Carriveau is nice?" Rylie fishes, wondering how much more Souliere will divulge about this intriguing Housemistress.

"*La meilleure!*" Souliere grins, proclaiming Miss Carriveau to be the very best. "*Mademoiselle Carriveau est merveilleuse!* You'll love her—everyone does. Just make sure you don't ... how to say it *en anglais* ..." She racks her brain for the right wording in English. "Tumble on her with love?"

Rylie snorts. "Fall in love with her?"

"*Oui! C'est ça!* That's it!"

"Why would I fall in love with her?"

Souliere shrugs. "You wouldn't be the first *fille en mal d'amour dans la maison de Carriveau*, and you don't want to end up with a broken neck like the last *ex-copine.*"

Rylie has trouble with a number of elements in that sentence. She wouldn't be the first girl in Carriveau's house to get lovesick over the Housemistress—that much she understands. But a broken neck? A poorly translated broken heart, she assumes. And *ex-copine*? The context suggests more than friendship. Ex-girlfriend? An exaggeration maybe.

She can think of at least fifteen different follow-up questions right off the bat, but doesn't get to voice even one before the bell rings and students spew into the hallways.

Chaos erupts.

CHAPTER TWO

MUCH TO RYLIE'S INCREASING FRUSTRATION, Souliere manages to drag out the tour for the entire day. They don't stop until dinnertime, when they head straight to the refectory for something to eat.

As per Missus Bursnell's rigid structuring of mealtimes, all students in years seven through eleven are required to eat breakfast, lunch, and dinner together in the refectory, as opposed to cooking for themselves in the kitchens of their respective houses, which the Lower and Upper Sixth students are allowed—and encouraged—to do.

The main doors to the refectory are closed to students at six o'clock sharp, and the children are served according to their year, beginning with Year Seven and ending with the sixth form. For tonight only, Rylie is permitted to sit with Souliere at the long bench table reserved for Year Eleven girls. In the future, if she wants to eat meals here, she'll take a place at the sixth form table instead.

Once they're all seated, another set of doors is opened to any members of the teaching staff who would rather eat here than go to the trouble of having to make their own evening meals, and they take their places in a separate area of the refectory, cordoned off from the student body by an ornate, wrought iron balustrade.

Barely listening to any of the conversations going on around her, Rylie keeps her eyes pinned to the faculty tables. The French woman is there, conversing with three other teachers, all speaking in heavily accented English, frequently slipping into either French or German, or something else entirely. They must represent the entire languages department, Rylie thinks, and they seem somewhat isolated from their peers. Apparently, even adults have cliques.

Rylie nudges Souliere with her elbow. "Is that Miss Carriveau?" She tips her head in the direction of the French woman.

"*Oui*." Souliere grins. "She's pretty, *non*?"

"When do I get to meet her?"

"I'll take you to her house soon, after we pick up the books you need from the library." She pronounces it lie-berry, drawing out the final syllable for an extra beat. "But be careful, *mon amie*, I think you have gooey eyes over her already."

Rylie wrinkles up her face, imagining eyeballs melting down her cheeks. "You what?"

"Gooey eyes," Souliere repeats. "How you say? *Les yeux de l'amour*?"

The eyes of love.

"Goo-goo eyes?" Rylie translates, diverting her gaze to her plate of food, unaware that she'd been staring. "You think I'm making goo-goo eyes at her?"

Souliere giggles. "It's okay. She's making them at you, too."

Sure enough, Rylie raises her eyes to the faculty tables once again and finds Carriveau looking right back at her. There's a reserved, slightly lopsided smile playing on her lips, almost cheeky, but not overtly so.

Rylie's heart thrums.

Arms laden with library books, Rylie follows Souliere inside one of the smaller boarding houses on the school grounds. They don't bother to knock.

The spacious halls echo with laughter and giggles, the strong, welcoming smell of baking drifting through the air. To the left of the main entrance, there's an open plan living area—the common room—complete with television, video games, beanbags, armchairs, and four sofas. To the right, there are three doors: one marked Carriveau, one marked Ansell, the other marked Study Room. In the center of the hall, a wide staircase leads up to the first floor, branching off left and right.

At the very back of the ground floor, there's a large kitchen. It has enough seating for just under forty people, three sinks, two ovens, five microwaves, and more pots and pans than Rylie's ever seen. Right now, the tables and counters are dusted with flour, fragments of egg shells, spilt milk, and the odd chocolate chip: they're baking cookies.

Students ranging from sixteen to eighteen are mixing, kneading, rolling, cutting, and appear to be having a great deal of fun in the process. Carriveau is there in the midst of it all, offering tips and guidance, making sure nobody puts their fingers near the blades of the electric whisks, or touches a power outlet with wet hands.

At the largest table, one of Carriveau's older—and least enthusiastic—pupils is kneading a powdery mixture in a bowl, barely dipping her fingers into it, afraid to make a mess.

"It's cold and gloopy," she complains, pulling a face.

Carriveau, the taller of the pair by more than a foot, swoops in behind the overly tentative young baker, leaving mere inches between them.

"It won't bite you, Varlow!" She laughs, grabbing the girl's hands and pushing them deep into the puddingy goop, forcing her to be much less delicate. "Work the ingredients together like this. See?" She manipulates Varlow's hands, cookie dough splurging between their entwined fingers. "You have to be firm!"

Varlow giggles. "It feels icky!"

"But it'll taste delicious." Carriveau kisses the side of her head.

It's chaste, brief, and motherly.

Announcing their presence, and the arrival of a newcomer into the fold, Souliere clears her throat, drawing Carriveau's concentration away from cookie making.

"*Mademoiselle Carriveau*"—she grabs Rylie by the sleeve of her cardigan and pulls her into the kitchen—"*voici la nouvelle fille, Rylie Harcourt.*"

Carriveau peels herself away from Varlow, doing so calmly and slowly. "*En anglais, Souliere.*" She wags a mildly disapproving, dough-covered finger at the eleventh year pupil, reminding her to speak English. "*Combien de fois l'ai-je répété? Vous devrez parler en anglais, même avec moi.*"

Rylie works the French over in her head: How many times must I repeat myself? You're required to speak English, even with me.

"*Pardonnez-moi, Mademoiselle.*" Immediately realizing she's made the same mistake twice, Souliere dips her head submissively. "I'm sorry, Miss."

Not in the mood to harp on the matter, Carriveau turns her attention on Rylie. In silence, she sucks raw cookie dough off one of her fingers, her cherry red lips wrapped around the slender digit, sliding from base to tip as she regards the pretty blonde with the same intense interest she'd shown earlier in the hallway.

Afterward, she flits her eyes back to Souliere. "Before you go, tell me what you think of this." She offers up another dough-encrusted finger.

The invitation is innocent enough.

Souliere takes a swipe of the sugary goodness on one of her own fingers and brings it to her mouth.

"It's good." She savors it. "Very sweet."

Before Rylie has a chance to wonder if she might be lucky enough to receive the same enticement, Carriveau's eyes are already back on her.

"Have you any allergies, Harcourt?"

Rylie shakes her head.

"Good." Carriveau holds the index finger of her other hand out. "So have a taste."

Noting that the proffered finger is being held at mouth level for her, Rylie steps forward and puts her lips around the base of the tendered digit, maintaining eye contact with Carriveau all the while, surprising the French woman with her boldness. When she gets to the tip, she flicks her tongue against Carriveau one last time, puckers her lips, and closes her mouth in the motion of a kiss, gently slipping away.

In the wake of it, lost in the sensuality of it all, she forgets to speak.

"Well?" Carriveau prompts her. "Do you like it?"

Eager to impress, Rylie calls upon some of the French she learnt at her old school, hoping she can string a few decent words together without sounding like a complete fool.

"*J'aime beaucoup cela.*" She licks remnants of dough off her lips. "*Merci.*"

I like it a lot, thank you.

Carriveau's mouth twitches, another smile trying to break free. "*Parlez-vous français?*"

"*Oui.*" Rylie squishes an inch of air between her thumb and forefinger, indicating a small amount of knowledge, not wanting to over-sell herself. "*Un peu.*"

Pinching the nail of her recently cleaned finger between her teeth, the moist fingertip resting on her lower lip, Carriveau finally lets the persistent smile escape.

"*Je vous aime bien, Harcourt.*" She follows that declaration with a translation, lest it should get misinterpreted. "I like you."

Rylie is transfixed on her lips. They look so soft; so kissable; so—

"Take her to my study," Carriveau directs Souliere, her command snapping Rylie out of a blossoming daydream. "I'll clean up and be right there."

Nodding compliantly, Souliere tugs on Rylie's cardigan again and leads her to the room marked Carriveau. Inside, there's a mahogany desk, cluttered with school books and test papers. One wall is completely covered by a custom-made bookshelf, while another is adorned with a small selection of Carriveau's educational certificates. She has a frigging PhD in English language and literature.

Rylie starts tallying things up: gorgeous, French, smart. How much better could this get?

"You want me to wait with you?" Souliere offers.

Rylie shakes her head. "I'll be fine. Thank you."

"Have fun, then." Souliere smirks. "*À bientôt!* See you soon! You're a Larkhillian now!"

Alone in Carriveau's study, Rylie sets her heavy books down on a leather sofa opposite the desk and begins to explore the bookshelf. Many of the books are, of course, about languages—including some that Rylie's never heard of. One of these looks similar to French, but it's called Occitan.

She fingers the spine of a book called *Occitan: A Beginner's Guide to Lenga d'Òc.* The book's author: Dr. Vivienne Carriveau.

Curious, she scoops the book off the shelf and flicks through it, becoming so absorbed in it that she doesn't hear the door open and close behind her.

"You have interest in languages?"

Carriveau's voice makes her jump.

"I'm sorry." She snaps the book shut, startled to find her Housemistress sneaking up on her. "I wasn't snooping. Honest."

"Don't be silly." Carriveau makes her hold up the book, revealing the subject of her fascination. "Books long to be read as we humans long to be loved. It is their *raison d'être, non?*"

24

"I suppose so." Rylie looks down at the book in her hands, curious to know what kind of language this is and why she's never heard of it. "What is Occitan?"

"It's a very old language from southern France. One of the Romance languages."

"A Romance language?" Rylie's never heard the term before.

"*Oui.*" Carriveau smiles, her eagerness to teach impossible to conceal. "Same as French, or Spanish, or Italian, which all derived from Vulgar Latin a long, long time ago. Unfortunately, Occitan is now rather endangered."

"Endangered?" Rylie imagines people stabbing dictionaries with tiny spears. "Like snow leopards and black rhinos?"

"In essence." Carriveau accepts the comparison. "Many of the people who speak it are advancing in their years, and if they don't pass on the language to the next generation—as my grandmother did with me—it will slowly become extinguished, like a candle's dying flame."

"That's so sad." Rylie slips the book back onto the shelf. "Are you fluent?" She realizes the stupidity of the question as soon as it leaves her lips. "I guess you must be." She reddens with embarrassment. "Can you say something to me in Occitan? I'd like to hear it."

"*Mais bien sûr!*" Carriveau beams, thrilled to be asked. "Of course! How about a poem?" She offers that rhetorically, locking on to Rylie's blues as she begins. "*Las! Qu'ieu d'Amor non ai conquis, mas cant lo trebalh e l'afan, ni res tant greu no·s covertis com fai so qu'ieu vau deziran. Ni tal enveja no·m fai res cum fai so qu'ieu non posc aver. Per una joja m'esbaudis fina, qu'anc re non amiey tan.*"

She pauses briefly to gauge Rylie's response, then continues.

"*Quan suy ab lieys si m'esbahis qu'ieu no·ill sai dire mon talan, e quan m'en vauc, vejaire m'es que tot perda·l sen e·l saber. Tota la genser qu'anc hom vis encontra lieys no pretz un guan. Quan totz lo segles brunezis, delai on ylh es si resplan."*

Reciting select verses from memory, she never once breaks eye contact.

"Dieu prejarai qu'ancar l'ades o que le vej'anar jazer. Totz trassalh e bran et fremis per s'Amor, durmen o velhan. Bel m'es quant ilh m'enfolhetis e·m fai badar e·n vau muzan! Qu'apres lo mal me venra bes be leu, s'a lieys ven a plazer." She stops and smiles. "Would you like to know what it means?"

Entranced, Rylie nods.

"Alas! I haven't gained, of love, but the torment and pain, for nothing is as hard to gain as that which I am seeking, nor any longing affects me as that for what I cannot have. I rejoice because of a pearl so fine that I never loved anything as much." Carriveau's heavy accent injects an extra layer of sensuality into words that are already brimming with feeling.

"When I am with her," she goes on, "I am so astonished that I don't dare vouch my desire, and when I part, it seems to me that I lose all my sense and my learning. The fairest woman one has ever seen, compared to her, isn't worth a glove. When the entire world turns to darkness, light shines from the place she rests."

She takes a deep breath, ostensibly affected by the beauty of the words even as they spill from her own lips, and when she moves into the last verse, a little heat rises into her cheeks.

"I shall pray God that I may touch her one day, or that I may see her go to bed. Awake or asleep, I quiver and am startled and shaken because of my love for her. It pleases me when she drives me insane, and makes me gape in stupor. For after the ill, the good will come. Soon, if such is her pleasure."

Silence descends.

She looks away, if only to hide her blush. "It was written by a twelfth century troubadour called Cercamon. Not much of his work has survived."

She moves toward her desk, leaving Rylie utterly dumbstruck and trying to wrap her head around what just transpired. Was that a poem? Or was that flirting? Maybe that's how people with doctorates in language and literature do it. After all, the private recital of some twelfth century poetry written in a dying language is bucket loads more romantic than your bog standard chat-up line.

"Come now." Carriveau breaks the silence, beckoning Rylie to the center of the room. "Let's take a proper look at you."

CHAPTER THREE

As RYLIE STANDS TO BE INSPECTED, SHE WATCHES A huddle of shadows gather on the other side of Carriveau's study door, well aware of what that means: they're being eavesdropped on.

Either not noticing or not caring, Carriveau continues undaunted, blatantly disregarding school policy once more as she takes Rylie by the shoulders and straightens her posture. "Shoulders back, head up." She hooks a finger under Rylie's chin, tilting her upwards. "Show off that pretty face."

Rylie does precisely as Carriveau asks, but not because she has any inclination to conform to the exacting standards of the school. She merely wants to prove that she does actually have a bust hidden beneath the baggy Larkhill cardigan that's hanging limply off her shoulders.

Indeed, Carriveau's eyes do spend quite a bit of time in that area. She flicks Rylie's hair off her shoulders, fussing with the shoulders of the cardigan, trying to get it to sit better.

"This does not fit you well," she concludes at last. "Take it off."

Rylie hesitates, scarcely able to believe she heard correctly.

Mistaking that hesitation for discomfort, Carriveau crosses the room to a large odds-and-sods cupboard and flings it open, simultaneously revealing a shelf full of spare Larkhill cardigans and her honorable intentions.

Not wanting Carriveau to think her coy, Rylie swiftly unbuttons the ugly cardigan and hands it over. "It's supposed to be my size."

"Hmm." Carriveau looks none too surprised. "Missus Bursnell likes a looser fit. I've long suspected that she has the staff who run the campus supply shop switch the labels."

"Does she have a problem with femininity?" Rylie wonders, catching a glimpse of her hair in a wall mirror, remembering Missus Bursnell's instruction to constrain it. "She told me I'm not to wear my hair loose like this."

"Shame," Carriveau mutters absently, checking the label on the cardigan and selecting one a size smaller from the cupboard. "It's unfortunate, but our esteemed Headmistress fears that sexuality is a distraction from scholarly endeavors."

"Yet she hired you." The words escape from Rylie's mouth before her brain has a chance to edit them. "I mean, you're so ..." She starts to backpedal, but she can tell by the wry smile on Carriveau's face that the retraction isn't necessary.

"It's true, the Headmistress and I share little but the desire to educate." Carriveau dangles the new cardigan on the end of her finger, closing the gap between them. "I've always felt that she would be best suited to a primary school environment, away from hormonal adolescents." She puts a finger to her lips, indicating silence. "But don't repeat that."

Rylie takes the cardigan and puts it on under the careful watch of Carriveau's eyes. This one fits perfectly, wrapping snugly around her breasts—which pleases them both.

"*Bien mieux*," Carriveau approves. "Much better." She swirls her finger in the air. "Now turn around, *s'il vous plaît*."

Rylie spins in a slow three-sixty, giving Carriveau ample time to continue the inspection of her uniform, starting with her shirt collar and tie, picking at a few minor things here and there.

"How old are you?" the Housemistress asks casually, crouching to check the hem of Rylie's skirt.

"Seventeen, Miss."

"Oh, really?" Carriveau sounds surprised. "That makes you the oldest girl in my Lower Sixth dorm, bar one other who's approaching eighteen also." She says that with a smile. "When's your birthday?"

"September—two days after the start of the school term. I'm always the oldest in my year and it sucks. I'll be almost nineteen by the time I finally graduate from the sixth form."

"Older is good," Carriveau mumbles to herself, pinching a loose thread between her fingers. "What classes are you taking?" She changes the subject without skipping a beat, giving the thread a gentle tug.

"English Language, Biology, and Psychology," Rylie answers proudly, her pride withering when she realizes that her selection no doubt precludes her from having the pleasure of being taught by Carriveau. "I was taking French as well, but I dropped out mid-way through last term," she adds, almost apologetically.

"*Quel dommage*; what a pity." Carriveau looks up at her, flashing a perfect set of pearly whites. "Never mind, I shall look forward to having you in one of my classes at least."

Rylie frowns, confused. "You teach English? Not French?"

"Both." The flawed stitching unravels in Carriveau's fingers. "Why did you drop out of French? It's such a shame. My sixth form French classes seem to get smaller and smaller every year."

Rylie looks needlessly rueful. "The AS-level French teacher at my old school was awful. I didn't like him at all." A thought runs through her mind. "Is it too late to change my enrollments?"

Carriveau's delicious red lips curl upwards again. "You've missed almost half a term. You'll have to promise me and Missus Bursnell that you'll make efforts to catch up with the rest of the class."

Rylie nods. "I can do that."

"And you might have to take extra lessons," Carriveau warns, winding the unraveled thread around her finger. "Maybe even some private tutoring."

That's meant as cautionary fodder for consideration, but it sounds like an invitation.

"With you?" Rylie clarifies, just to be sure.

"*Oui*," the arresting French woman answers with a smile, her fingers still at work.

"In that case," Rylie concludes, "I wouldn't mind at all."

"Very well, then." Carriveau pulls the thread taut. "I'll see to it first thing in the morning. I sincerely hope you won't tire of looking at me, though. Having me here after classes, and in English, and French, and private lessons ... we'll be seeing a lot of one another."

As she says that, she leans forward to break off the offending thread, giving Rylie a clear view down her blouse—albeit fleetingly. In a second, she's back on her feet, retrieving a needle and thread from the supply cupboard.

"It's strange that you were transferred from your old school so abruptly in the middle of a term," she muses, dropping to her knees again at Rylie's feet, sewing tools in hand. "Did you have problems there?"

Rylie shrugs. "My parents thought so."

"Are you troublesome, Harcourt?" Carriveau asks with a smirk.

"I don't think so, Miss."

"That's just as well." Carriveau slips on her reading glasses and threads the needle. "I'm many things, but a disciplinarian is not one of them. This house is run on mutual trust and respect. I set clear boundaries, and I expect you to adhere to them at all times. If you can do that, I daresay we'll get along."

Kneeling closer than before, she takes the hem of Rylie's skirt in her hands and flips it up to expose the underside so that she can begin stitching. Her face is at crotch height, and Rylie can feel body heat radiating from her as she works. Every now and again, a subtle draft drifts beneath her lifted skirt, cooling the gusset of her knickers, evaporating some of the moisture there.

She's aroused, and awkwardly so. Hoping that Carriveau can't smell how uncontrollably horny she is, the throbbing between her legs making her increasingly anxious, she clutches two fistfuls of her skirt, wiping her clammy palms off on the soft cotton.

Carriveau peers up at her over the rim of the reading glasses, aware of a shift in her disposition. "*Êtes-vous nerveuse, mon chou?*"

Rylie's distracted brain struggles with the simple language conversion: Are you nervous, my cabbage? Being called a cabbage is momentarily disturbing, until she recalls her parents' French housekeeper calling her that when she was a child. Ergo, it's an old-fashioned term of endearment.

"*Non, Madame,*" she lies, finally responding.

"*Madame?*" Carriveau briefly stops stitching. "*Mademoiselle, s'il vous plaît. Je suis célibataire.*" She focuses back on the needle and thread.

"*Célibataire?*" Rylie assumes there's more to the translation than the seemingly obvious.

"It means unmarried, not celibate," Carriveau explains. "Although, it has to be said, I'm finding it increasingly difficult to tell the difference."

Whether she's fishing for flattery or not, Rylie pounces on the opportunity to dish some out.

"*C'est tragique,*" she offers condolences for her Housemistress's marital state, then returns the compliment given to her earlier in the foyer. "*Tu es belle, Mademoiselle Carriveau.*"

Carriveau arches an eyebrow, secretly pleased that Rylie finds her attractive. "*Je suis flattée, ma chère.*" She looks up, gauging Rylie's understanding of the French, offering an English translation just in case. "I'm flattered."

There's a pair of scissors in the cupboard, but instead of fetching them when she gets to the end of the seam, Carriveau finishes off the stitching and bends forward to cut the thread with her teeth, sending Rylie's hormones into overdrive.

It's all the teen can do to withhold a gasp, biting on her lower lip as Carriveau's warm breath tickles her bare thigh, making her skin prick with goose bumps.

"There." Carriveau rocks back on her heels, admiring her handiwork, seemingly unaware of Rylie's sexual excitement. "Good as new."

She lifts the reading glasses back onto the top of her head, but doesn't yet retreat. Instead, she places a hand on Rylie's hip and runs it down over her thigh and rump several times, smoothing out some slight, barely visible creases in the skirt, pressing firmly, molding her hand to fit the contours of Rylie's body.

"This could use an iron, *non*?"

Rylie feels a tiny shiver ripple through her core. Her beautiful French Housemistress just totally copped a feel! The astonishing moment of quasi-permissible intimacy doesn't last, though. A stern female voice startles the eavesdroppers outside the door, causing the shadows to scatter. Shortly thereafter, there's a knock.

"*Entrez!*" Carriveau calls out, still on her knees.

The woman who enters is several years older than Carriveau. There are flecks of gray in her done-up auburn hair, her face bears some lines of age, and she's started to widen around the mid-region. Her ankle-length, tie-die skirt belongs in a decade far removed from this one, and her bobbly sweater is at least one size too big.

Caught off-guard by Carriveau's position on the floor in front of Rylie, she hovers in the doorway, not knowing quite where to cast her eyes. "Pardon my intrusion."

Wholly unconcerned, Carriveau gets to her feet, accepting the hand Rylie offers to help her off the floor.

"Miss Ansell, we have a new student." She squeezes Rylie's hand before letting go. "This is Rylie

Harcourt." She takes Rylie by the shoulder and pushes her forward, presenting her to the frumpy woman. "Harcourt, this is Miss Ansell, Deputy Housemistress and teacher of geography."

Miss Ansell smiles politely at Rylie, then gets on with business. "It's almost nine-thirty." She consults her watch to be certain. "Should I show Harcourt to the dorm?"

"*Ce n'est pas nécessaire.*" Carriveau dismisses the suggestion with a flick of her wrist. "I can do it. If you wouldn't mind, though, could you check on the kitchen? Some of the children and I were baking cookies before I was drawn away."

"As you wish." Miss Ansell appears reluctant to go, but doesn't argue.

"We have two dormitories here," Carriveau explains as she leads Rylie up the staircase. "One for the Lower Sixth, and one for the older girls in the Upper Sixth. While I am responsible for the house overall, Miss Ansell helps out with the Upper Sixth—doing bed checks, wake-ups, and so on—and she's in charge of the house when I'm not here."

At the top of the stairs, the hallway branches off left and right: Upper Sixth dormitory to the left, Lower Sixth dormitory to the right, bathrooms adjacent to each. Miss Ansell's private quarters, Carriveau points out, are located at the far end of the Upper Sixth hallway, while her own are located at the end of the Lower Sixth hallway.

As she stops at a large linen cupboard to collect fresh bed sheets and a duvet cover, Rylie breaks away from her to examine the many and varied framed photographs hanging on the walls.

Some are house pictures, with Carriveau and Miss Ansell standing proudly with their students from one year to the next. As with most school pictures, there are always one or two students who ruin an otherwise perfect shot by looking in the wrong place at the wrong time, and last year's photograph is no exception. One of the Lower Sixth girls has her head turned partially to the side, her eyes fixed on something that was obviously far more interesting than the photographer.

Rylie squints, trying to follow her sightline. She appears to have her eyes locked on Carriveau, as does one of the other girls—and *that* girl Rylie recognizes. She's the rather bedraggled student who came to Carriveau's rescue in the lobby.

Going back beyond three full school years, there's a different Housemistress and Rylie loses interest. Other pictures are from various sporting events, where the houses are pitted against one another to promote friendly competition. Lacrosse appears to be a particular favorite, and one of the most recent pictures is of a sporty blonde bearing Carriveau house colors—purple and gold—holding up a trophy.

Kaitlyn Simmons.

Team Captain.

Most Valuable Player.

"Do you play?" Carriveau wonders, looking fondly at the picture, hugging an armful of lavender scented linens to her chest. "I get the impression you might be rather athletic."

Rylie's stomach performs a little somersault. That impression was obviously gleaned from caressing her firm ass and muscular thighs, thus confirming her suspicion that the tactile exploration of her body had bugger all to do with the wrinkles in her uniform.

"Lacrosse is my main sport, but I'm no MVP," she answers modestly, electricity shooting through her as Carriveau's shoulder brushes against hers. "How many girls are there here?"

"Our capacity is thirty, but as of this moment, we have twenty-seven: fifteen in the Upper Sixth and twelve in the Lower Sixth, with one Head Girl in each dormitory." Carriveau swings open the door into the Lower Sixth dorm.

The long, wide room has been partitioned off into fifteen equal cubicles, the dividing walls only four and a half feet high. This gives the girls privacy while sleeping, but allows Carriveau to look in on them easily.

Each cubicle is rectangular, precisely long enough for a single bed to fit snugly against one wall—completely boxed in on three sides—and wide enough to accommodate a bedside table that has one lockable drawer in which to keep any valuables and private items, a small dresser, and a twenty-four inch clothing rail on the back wall for hanging uniforms. Besides those few things, there's little else: a waste paper basket, a lamp, and a small mirror on the wall above the table.

"It's not much." Carriveau reads Rylie's expression of discontent perfectly, showing her to the third cubicle on the right. "But you can decorate it however you'd like. You'll find some Blu-Tack in the bedside drawer. No pins, *s'il vous plaît.*"

Rylie glances at some of the others, finding the walls cluttered with everything from shirtless male models to glitter hearts and unicorns. A smaller percentage of the girls have opted for tasteful magazine cutouts of their favorite actors and musicians, while fewer still have completely nude female pin-ups tacked to the walls beside their beds, bare nipples and vaginas covered by stickers.

One particularly brave girl has even created her own personal masturbation material. She's filled an entire wall of her cubicle with numerous hand-drawn pictures of a Carriveau-esque female: dark hair, green eyes, long legs. Many of them show her with an exaggerated, cartoonish bust, offering maximum cleavage, breasts threatening to burst out from the confines of tight clothing.

"That's Adel Edwards' cubicle." Carriveau catches Rylie gawping at the artwork and steers her back toward her own space. "She can be somewhat extreme."

Adel Edwards? Rylie lets the name percolate for a moment. Edwards, Edwards, Edwards ... the girl Carriveau was talking to the in the lobby? The girl in last year's Lower Sixth house photograph? Shouldn't she be in the Upper Sixth by now? Unless ...

"She's repeating Year Twelve?" It's the only conclusion Rylie can draw. "That explains why I'm not quite the oldest girl in your dorm."

Carriveau tilts her head, one eyebrow raised, silently questioning.

"I recognized her in last year's Lower Sixth house picture," Rylie explains. "She's the girl I saw you with earlier, isn't she? I heard you use her name." She glances back at the boobie pictures. "Don't you mind that she's objectifying you?"

"It's a fantasy. It's perfectly normal." Carriveau shrugs it off as insignificant. "Have you never had a crush on a teacher before?"

Rylie's blush says it all.

Her cheeks are burning with a fury more intense than the Great Fire of London, though not for the crushes she's had in the past, but for the one she's developing right now.

Averting her eyes, she steps inside her cubicle, finding a duvet folded neatly on the floor, a pillow atop it, and her suitcase on the bed. Missus Bursnell must've had someone bring it here from her office. While she explores, Carriveau stands patiently at the cubicle entryway, still nursing the linens.

Eventually, "Could you take these?" The patient Housemistress holds them out. "I can't reach the bed."

Rylie looks down, finding the toes of Carriveau's stilettos connecting with a strip of yellow electrical tape that marks the cubicle boundary.

"Are you a vampire? Do I have to invite you in?"

"Impossible, I'm afraid." Carriveau shakes her head. "Your cubicle is the one place on school premises that belongs entirely to you. Within it, you have complete privacy, and I'm not permitted to enter—even at your invitation."

"That's no fun." Rylie takes the sheets and sets them on the bed.

"Of course," Carriveau adds a quick caveat to the rule, "if I suspect that you're breaking school regulations and hiding contraband, I have the right to conduct a search of your cubicle in the presence of another staff member."

"Contraband?" Rylie heaves her suitcase up onto the dresser, moving it out of the way so that she can make her bed unimpeded. "What kind of contraband?"

Carriveau shrugs. "Drugs, alcohol, cigarettes, weapons, fireworks, pornography."

"Porn?" Rylie pulls a face. "Are you pulling my leg?" She shakes out the fitted sheet and lays it over the mattress. "What harm could some nudie pics do?"

"Missus Bursnell doesn't approve."

Rylie rolls her eyes, expecting no less from the withered, one-eyed hag. "All the problems in the world, and she's worried about teenage girls having orgasms."

"*Exactement.*" Carriveau leans on the cubicle wall, sighing. "It's thoroughly ridiculous." She pauses, giving some thought to what she says next. "Perhaps the old woman's bitter because she's not having any of her own."

Rylie's jaw drops, not quite able to believe that Carriveau would say something like that about the Headmistress—and so candidly, too! It's both shocking and refreshing, and the frank turn this conversation is taking triggers her to blurt out:

"I have a dildo in my suitcase."

If Carriveau is shocked by the unprompted confession, she hides it exceedingly well.

"Really?" she asks casually, her tone neutral.

"Uh-huh." Rylie unzips her suitcase. "Do you want to confiscate it?"

"*Non,*" Carriveau answers without giving the matter any thought, thus affirming her stance in opposition of Larkhill's moral war on sexuality. "I daresay you'll need it. If you've read the student handbook, you'll know that engaging in sexual relations with anyone on campus—including your peers—is strictly prohibited."

"Why?" Rylie steps away from the suitcase, her stomach fluttering. "Because we're all girls?"

Carriveau chooses her words with great care, answering slowly. "The Headmistress deems such activity ... inappropriate."

Rylie mulls that over. Is it sex Missus Bursnell doesn't approve of? Or lesbianism? She turns her focus back to the bed. Not knowing precisely where to begin, she pulls the fitted sheet over the near bottom corner, then over the near top, then realizes she has to take off her shoes and clamber onto the bed to complete the task.

In doing so, crawling clumsily over the sheet, smoothing it as she goes, she feels her skirt ride up in the back. Wondering if Carriveau might be inclined to sneak a peek at her thighs while she's in this position, she contorts herself to look at the mirror, hoping to get a glimpse of Carriveau's reflection—and she's not disappointed.

Carriveau, still leaning on the cubicle wall, her chin resting on the heel of her palm, propped up on her elbow, isn't even trying to be discreet. While her facial expression is tightly controlled—neither revealing arousal nor apathy—her eyes are most definitely engaged, taking mental snapshots of the view.

Taunting her audience deliberately, Rylie spreads her legs a little, making it appear as though she's doing so to help anchor the sheet with her knees. Bending forward, she lowers the front of her body and slips the sheet over the farthest corner of the mattress.

She can't see into the mirror anymore, but she's certain she must be holding Carriveau's interest. Staying in this position for as long as possible, on her knees and elbows, bent completely over the bed, her ass barely covered, she delights in how naughty this feels.

Ping!

The fitted sheet slips off the bottom corner.

40

"Damn it," she grumbles, turning around to force it back.

When she does that, the top corner makes a bid for freedom, the sheet only getting more tangled beneath her as she attempts to straighten everything back out.

Carriveau covers her mouth with her hand, trying to suppress a laugh. What began as a moderately erotic spectacle is quickly turning into a farce.

Rylie fixes both bottom corners again and yanks the top up to the other end of the mattress, not realizing that one of the bottom corners is already starting to slip. While she makes a valiant effort to get one of the upper corners in place, Carriveau lunges forward to catch the bottom corner, snagging it before it can pop free.

Feeling movement behind her, Rylie spins to attack the bottom corner again, only to come face to face with Carriveau, almost smacking heads.

"*Putain!*" Carriveau exclaims, startled by Rylie's agility, recoiling slightly to avoid being accidentally head-butted.

She's bent forward, one foot outside the yellow boundary line and one foot within. She has one hand on the fitted sheet, the other clutching the footboard for balance, and from her vantage point lower down on the bed, almost splayed out on the sheet, Rylie can see straight down her blouse—a much closer look than she'd gotten earlier.

She lets her eyes drop ... then raises them back up, cocking her head. "Wait, did you just call me a whore?"

"*Non! Certainement pas!*" Carriveau lets go of the sheet and makes a swift retreat from the bed.

"Aww, shit." Rylie pouts, the sheet hitting her in the face.

"Have you never made a bed before?" Carriveau straightens her blouse, trying to forge the illusion that everything going on here is perfectly innocent and above board.

"No." Rylie frowns apologetically, her limbs all caught up in the sheet. "We have a maid at home."

She rolls over onto her side, kicking to get loose. In the process, she leans over the edge of the bed, glancing down at Carriveau's feet—both of which are now way beyond the thin yellow line.

"Uh-oh." She points at them. "Where do I have to go to report you for that?"

She's joking, of course, but despite the lighthearted intent, Carriveau scowls, reaches for Rylie's hand, and pulls her up.

"Off the bed!" she orders in a hushed voice. "Now!" She ushers her out of the cubicle.

"What are you doing?"

"What your mother should've done a long time ago." She snatches the fitted sheet and gets it on the bed in the first try, hooking the farthest corners over the mattress first. "Pay attention now."

With genuine interest, Rylie watches her turn the duvet cover completely inside out, put her hands inside to grab the top corners, then grab the corresponding top corners of the duvet, shaking the cover down over it.

"*Voilà!*" She buttons up the end and spreads it out on the bed. "*Fini!*" She switches places with Rylie, giving her a gentle shove into the cubicle as she crosses back over the yellow line. "Now, housekeeping comes in to change bed sheets weekly, and the bins daily. No food is allowed in your cubicle. You're responsible for your own laundry, unless you need something dry cleaned, then you tag it, bag it, and leave it for the matron to pick up—she comes by every Wednesday. Mail is held at a central mailroom; it's your responsibility to report there and collect it at least once a week.

"You're expected to brush your teeth twice a day, shower daily, and keep your hair clean. I'm sure Missus Bursnell's already gone over the rest." Carriveau starts backing away, rushing through her mental checklist. "Bedtime is ten o'clock on school nights, and eleven o'clock on Fridays and Saturdays. Lights out after fifteen minutes." She checks her watch to confirm the current time. "Now unpack and get ready for bed. I'll return to say goodnight."

With that, she leaves.

CHAPTER FOUR

TEETH BRUSHED, BELONGINGS PUT AWAY, NAIL polish scrubbed off, Rylie sits on the edge of her bed in a pair of thin cotton pajamas, watching a tiny spider crawl across the floor of her cubicle. While all around her the other girls in her dormitory giggle and joke and get themselves ready for bed, she tries earnestly to recall every bit of dialogue exchanged between herself and Carriveau.

She'd gone too far—that much is obvious. Was it looking down her blouse that did it? Or making that daft crack about reporting her for stepping over the line? Whichever straw it was that proved to be the last one, Carriveau's disposition had done a swift one-eighty, transitioning from casually flirtatious to strained austerity in a heartbeat.

"Uck!" She jerks her bare foot, flinging off the wandering spider.

Responding to her utterance of revulsion, a head pops up over the adjoining cubicle wall. An untamed bob of curly red hair frames a pale, freckled face, hazel eyes gleaming with youthful excitement at the sight of a potential new friend.

"What's your name?" The girl grins, propping her elbows on the dividing wall.

"Rylie."

"I'm Gabrielle. Gabby, if you like." The girl thrusts her right hand over the wall. "Why do you look sad? Is this your first time away from home?"

Rylie shakes her head and Gabby's proffered hand. "I think I upset Miss Carriveau."

"Already?" Gabby snorts. "How did you manage that?"

"I don't always think before I speak."

"Congratulations, you're a teenager." Gabby laughs heartily. "I 'spect our good old house mum's well used to it, though." She peers over the cubicle wall at Rylie's belongings, leaning so far forward that she almost falls in. "Where are you from?"

"Canterbury, Kent."

"Crikey! You're a long way from home! Mum and dad keen to get rid of ya?"

"Keen to whip me into shape, more like."

"Ooh." Gabby's eyes widen. "Are you a bad 'un?"

Rylie chuckles. "Yeah, I'm such a bad influence. You'd best stay well clear. My intolerance of parental bullshit might be contagious."

Cutting their conversation short, Carriveau returns to the dormitory—as promised, at fifteen minutes on the dot—her arms full of books. She begins on the left side of the room and makes her way down the row of cubicles, checking each one in turn, making sure everything is in order before signalling her approval with a nod of her head and a succinct goodnight.

She speaks in English until she reaches a German exchange student, whereupon she slips seamlessly into the girl's first language and instructs her to hang up her school uniform before turning in for the night.

Afterward, "*Gute nacht, Gersten.*"

"*Gute nacht, Fraulein Carriveau.*"

Two cubicles down, Carriveau finds a lacy pink thong in the middle of the aisle. She hooks it onto the toe of her shoe and dangles it in the air.

"Yours?" She offers it to the girl in the nearest cubicle.

The undergarment is quickly snatched up.

Carriveau reaches the end of the aisle and makes her way down the other side of the room, offering only one reprimand for some spilt glittery nail polish, expressing grave disapproval that the mess hadn't been cleaned up before it dried, but making no mention of the fact that it's expressly forbidden. As she approaches Rylie's cubicle, her already waning smile tightens.

"Harcourt, you left these in my study." She holds out the bundle of books she's been cradling. "If you need anything, don't be afraid to come to me," she goes on, her paper burden lifted. "My door is always open."

Her words express tenderness, but her tone implies indifference. Perhaps the latter is intended to conceal the true depth of the former, but the more she talks, the more tenderness seems to win out, causing an underwear-clad Adel Edwards to glare at Rylie from her cubicle on the other side of the room.

"I know it can be a difficult transition for a girl who's never boarded before, but I will endeavor to do everything in my power to make sure you leave this institution with fond memories of your time here." Carriveau's eyes never leave Rylie's. "Do you think that will be possible?"

Rylie can't stop her cheeks from flushing. "I should think so, Miss."

"Good. Happy girls make a happy house, which makes for an exceedingly happy Housemistress." With a smile that seems only slightly forced, Carriveau turns her attention to Gabby. "Laurenson, you'll take care of Harcourt tomorrow, won't you? You have several of the same classes."

Gabby, still kneeling on her bed, leaning over the cubicle wall, nods. "Yuppers."

"I'll let your other teachers know that you'll be helping her out for the next two or three days, so if you're a few minutes late here and there, you won't be marked down for it."

Gabby beams. "*Carte blanche!*"

Carriveau rolls her eyes theatrically, returning her attention briefly to Rylie. "Goodnight, Harcourt."

"*Bonne nuit, Mademoiselle.*"

Rylie can't be certain, but as Carriveau turns away, she seems to let a genuine smile escape. Has their earlier moment of impropriety now been forgiven?

Carriveau completes her arc around the room, turns out the lights, and steps into the hallway, the rhythmic sound of her footsteps slowly fading. Still, Rylie can't shake the feeling that she should apologize for her impudent behavior. In particular, for the lewd posturing and the cheeky taunts. Unable to get into bed without clearing the air, she tiptoes out of her cubicle and pads barefoot into the hallway, the dormitory door creaking on its hinges.

Already halfway to her private quarters, Carriveau comes to an abrupt stop.

The hallway falls silent.

Her back to the dormitory, the Housemistress offers no movement but the slight turn of her head, waiting for the student to announce herself.

"*Mademoiselle Carriveau.*" Rylie's quiet voice reverbs in the sterile corridor.

"That was quick." Carriveau pivots, otherwise staying put. "Is there something amiss?"

Rylie lowers her gaze to the floor, wiggling her toes. The linoleum tiles are cold against her bare feet, but nothing in the world could be as frigid as Carriveau's icy demeanor in this moment. Not even the Arctic tundra. Was chasing her out into the hallway yet another wrong move? Too much eagerness? Desperation? Too late now.

"I ... I'm afraid I've done something to upset you." Feeling uncharacteristically teary, Rylie dare not look up for fear of being utterly crushed by those hardened emerald eyes.

Barely a second passes before Carriveau melts. Her expression softens, and she strides back toward the dorm, her hands outstretched.

"*Non, ma chère. Pas du tout.*" She sweeps Rylie's hair out of her face and thumbs her cheeks. "Not at all. Why ever would you think that?" She keeps Rylie's head tilted up, cupping her chin, slender fingers pressed to her neck.

"Earlier, you left the dorm so suddenly." Rylie sniffles. "I thought I must've done something wrong. I was joking when I said I'd report you for—"

"I know." Carriveau smiles reassuringly. "You did nothing wrong, sweetheart." She moves her hands up, holding Rylie's head, fingers weaving through her hair. "Absolutely nothing. I was the one who conducted myself poorly."

"No." Rylie would shake her head, but she's being held too firmly. "You were only helping me, I—"

"Hush." Carriveau presses a soft fingertip to the teen's bare pink lips, letting it rest there for a moment. "It was improper, and that's all there is to it."

Her finger slips away and she extricates herself from Rylie's personal space, taking a small step back. "Now you must get to bed. I can't make exceptions."

That word rebounds from brain cell to brain cell in Rylie's mind. Exceptions? What sort of exceptions? Relaxing the curfew? To her ear, Carriveau's cryptic assertion sounds more like the reiteration of a mantra than it does a simple warning to a new pupil. As a recovering alcoholic might look at themselves in the mirror each morning and say "I will not drink today," so Rylie can picture Carriveau repeating quietly to herself, "I can't make exceptions."

Convincing herself of this fact—and that she hadn't imagined the faint undercurrent of determination in her Housemistress's voice—Rylie heads for the dormitory, wondering what rules Carriveau might be tempted to break.

As she reaches the door ...

"Rylie," Carriveau purrs out her name. "Wait."

Obediently, Rylie halts, her hand on the knob. She can hear Carriveau's stiletto heels clicking on the linoleum behind her, and by the time she spins around, she finds herself practically backed up against the dormitory door.

Without saying a word, Carriveau places her steady hands back on either side of the dumbstruck teen's head and brings her forward, pressing a chaste kiss on her forehead.

"*Bonne nuit, mon ange*," she whispers, her eyes roving over Rylie's features somewhat reverently. "*Fais de beaux rêves.*"

Rylie shivers as Carriveau calls her an angel and wishes her sweet dreams. All too soon, though, she feels the warmth of Carriveau's touch dissipate, leaving her with nothing but the lingering sensation of those deep red, lipstick-coated lips.

"Don't forget to look at your books," Carriveau says in parting. "Make sure I didn't forget anything."

Rylie nods, watching Carriveau walk away, her skirt clinging to her delightfully spankable *derrière*, then she slips back inside the dorm, tiptoeing quietly to her bed, trying to draw as little attention as possible.

Once in her cubicle, she retrieves her stack of library books off the floor and—using her cell phone as a light source—sorts through them, setting aside those she knows she'll need for tomorrow's lessons.

At the bottom of the pile, she finds a paperback that lacks a Larkhill Boarding School library sticker on the spine. Curious, she flips it over.

Her heart drums inside her chest. It's the Occitan book from Carriveau's study, and the first page has a freshly-inked inscription:

Rylie,

Explore your interest.

V.

Sleep doesn't come easy. Rylie lies awake, listening to the creaks and groans of the building, the woodwork expanding and contracting in response to heat or cold, the pipes complaining as somewhere, someone in the building makes a demand for water.

Soon enough, there's another noise keeping her awake.

"Oh, *Mademoiselle* ..." a soft, girlish voice mewls in the darkness.

Rylie holds her breath, listening for more. A dream, perhaps?

"Oh, Vivienne ..." the voice whispers frantically. "Yes! More!"

Nope, definitely not a dream.

The voice is quiet, but distinct: it's Adel Edwards.

Bed sheets ruffle and hit the floor, kicked off the bed no doubt.

"Oh, I'm going to come ..."

No fucking way! Rylie peels back the covers on her own bed and rises slowly to her knees, peering into the shadowy room beyond her rectangle of private space. To her right, there's a giggle: two of the other Lower Sixth girls are making out beneath the covers. To her left, there's Adel Edwards ... completely alone.

Rylie stifles a chuckle. Adel is lying on her back, her nightdress bunched up, legs spread, both hands vigorously working between her legs.

"Oh, fuck me!" she begs huskily, her eyes closed, her breathing labored. "I'm gonna come so hard for you ..."

And she does.

As her climax hits, Rylie turns away, afraid of letting out a guffaw. She's about to flop back down in her bed when a flicker of light catches her attention.

Left on for safety's sake, in case anyone needs to venture out to use the bathroom in the middle of the night, dim yellow hallway lights illuminate a two-inch crack beneath the dormitory door, and at this moment, the warm glow seeping through is broken by the movement of a shadowy figure on the other side.

Feet.

Ankles.

There's someone standing near the door, leaning against the doorjamb.

Rylie squints at the shifting shapes, making out the thin bar of a stiletto heel. It couldn't be, could it? Miss Carriveau? Listening to Adel Edwards masturbate? Holy shit!

Rylie strains to hear anything beyond Adel's orgasm. Is Carriveau touching herself out there? Is she horny? What *is* she doing?! Was she just walking by and happened to overhear her name uttered in the heat of sexual fervor? Did curiosity compel her to stay?

Whatever the case, in the wake of Adel's climax, Carriveau slinks away, the shadows receding as the house quiets back down to its usual nocturnal rhythm of distant clangs and clatterings, a squirrel scratching away in the attic.

Bonne nuit, en effet!

Good night, indeed!

CHAPTER FIVE

CARRIVEAU RUNS HER HANDS OVER HER HIPS, flattening her skintight skirt over her thighs. Is it too much? No, she shakes her head, dismissing the thought. This is one of her favorite suits. It's formfitting, but not obscenely short. It more than covers the lacy tops of her stockings, which she wears simply for her own self-esteem rather than for any practical purpose.

The stockings, like the stilettos and the push-up bra, make her feel elegant and feminine, reminding her that she's still a sexual being, despite the fact that her only bedmates of late have been battery powered.

Taking a deep breath, she adjusts the open collar of her blouse and applies a new shade of lipstick, counting down the final seconds until the commencement of the usual morning pandemonium.

"No exceptions," she reminds her reflection, then walks briskly from her study, striding boldly into the Lower Sixth dormitory not a minute later.

"*Réveillez-vous!*" She claps her hands several times, making the slap of her palms as loud as possible. "Come on, girls! Wakey-wakey!" She glides down the aisle, leaning over to tug the corner of a duvet off one sleeping girl. "*Lève-toi, Mademoiselle Brody.*" She points a finger at another reluctant waker. "*Toi aussi, Petersen.*"

A cacophony of chatter quickly erupts, Carriveau paying no note to the fact that two of the Lower Sixth girls rise from the same bed. When she arrives at Rylie's cubicle, she finds the newcomer lying prone, her pillow pulled over her face, one of her bare feet poking out from the bottom of the duvet.

"Up you get, sleepyhead." Carriveau bends forward and grabs that exposed foot, shaking it gently.

Rylie groans, but does as she's told.

"How was your first night with us?" Carriveau leans on the cubicle wall, her open collar shirt showing even more cleavage than yesterday.

"Very good, Miss." Rylie sits up and yawns, ruffling a hand through her blonde mane.

"You're feeling better about things this morning, I hope?" Carriveau's eyes dart over to the bedside table, where the Occitan book is sitting proudly and prominently.

"A great deal." Rylie rises to her knees to stretch, enjoying the view in front of her. *"Merci, Mademoiselle."*

From this higher position, she can see two girls in the cubicle behind Carriveau. They're whispering to one another, ogling her bum. After first wondering how they could be so openly disrespectful, she realizes Carriveau can see their reflections in the cubicle mirror. If she were so inclined, she could chastise them. She doesn't.

"Today, I'll make you breakfast," she carries on her conversation with Rylie perfectly naturally, as if unaware of her admirers. "Tomorrow onward, you can fend for yourself in the mornings. How does that sound?"

Rylie takes a moment to think, composing her words carefully so as not to make a mistake when she tells Carriveau how perfect that sounds. *"Cela me semble parfait."*

Judging by the curve of Carriveau's lips, her diction is perfect, too.

"You're quite adorable, Harcourt. Do you always make this much effort to impress your teachers?"

"No," Rylie answers frankly, shuffling closer. "Do you always offer to make breakfast for the new girl?"

"Of course." Carriveau pushes herself away from the cubicle wall. "Now hurry down." She walks out of the dormitory without glancing back. "I hope you like toast."

In the hallway, Carriveau weaves through a gaggle of half-naked, squealing girls with a broad smile pinned on her face. In contrast, Miss Ansell, who's standing at the top of the staircase, refereeing between two Upper Sixth girls who're fighting over a towel, looks as though she's already reaching the end of a rapidly shortening tether—and it's only seven o'clock.

She settles the dispute, sends the girls off to the bathroom, and drinks in Carriveau's appearance: the closely fitted suit, the bright eyes, the upturned lips, and the palpable vivacity exuding from her.

"You look unusually cheery this morning," she remarks, roaming her eyes from ankles to hair, a hint of suspicion in her voice.

"Because it's a wonderful morning." Carriveau beams, skipping down the stairs.

She's the first one in the kitchen, and as she fusses around the room gathering bread, a plate, and a knife, she hums a song to herself, oblivious to the fact that she acquires a spectator halfway through the second verse.

"Since when do you have toast for breakfast?"

Miss Ansell's voice makes her jump.

"It's not for me." She drops two slices of bread into the toaster. "It's for the new girl."

"Oh, aye? And when did we start doing that?" Miss Ansell folds her arms, her hands almost completely covered by the long sleeves of her baggy purple sweater.

Carriveau doesn't reply.

"She's a very pretty little thing, isn't she?" The Deputy Housemistress continues to needle her colleague. "In fact, I reckon she looks a fair bit like our old Kaitlyn Simmons. You agree?"

Carriveau replies with a dispassionate shrug, feigning nonchalance. "I hadn't noticed."

Miss Ansell chortles, slumping against the countertop. "You must think I'm daft. I haven't seen you this chipper since—"

Carriveau smacks the butt of the knife down on the counter. "That's enough!" she barks at the Deputy Housemistress. "I'm in a good mood, that's all. There's no need to ruin it."

Miss Ansell edges nearer, peering up at Carriveau's taut mouth. "Is that a new shade of lipstick I see on those angry lips?" She moves away from the counter, ready to make her own breakfast. "Watch yourself, Vivienne."

When she says Carriveau's name, it sounds harsh and angular: Vih-vee-uhn. To hear it squawked at her that way makes Carriveau feel like a naughty little girl being reprimanded by her British nanny.

"*Vivienne, s'il te plaît,*" she purrs out her own name, her heavy accent and soft inflection making each syllable sound warm and smooth.

Vi.vjen.

In the next moment, Rylie enters the kitchen. Arriving before any of the other girls—having rushed through her morning routine for that very reason—she's clearly cut some corners with her appearance. Her shirt's only half tucked in, her skirt's twisted sideways, her cardigan's buttoned improperly, and her hair is bound in a messy braid.

Carriveau—her good mood restored by the teen's arrival—suppresses laughter. Rylie's hair is sticking up on top, two big tufts bunched near her crown, having nearly missed inclusion into the braid altogether. The sides are twisted, wrenched carelessly into chunks and tugged back to form the outer strands at the top of the off-center braid, which itself is so loose that some of the shorter sections of hair are already falling out of it.

"Is that the best you could do?" Carriveau beckons her over for a closer inspection.

"Does it look terrible?" Rylie supposes that it must. "This was my third attempt."

Carriveau spins her around, checking to see if it can be salvaged. "Have you never braided your own hair before?"

"I've never braided *any* hair. I had to Google it."

"*Tu es si mignonne.*" Carriveau pats her shoulder, amused that a seventeen-year-old girl could get this far in life without learning such a simple thing. "You're so cute."

With that, she presses a kiss against Rylie's head, as she'd done to the girl named Varlow last night when they were making cookies. Then, she pulls a chair out at the table.

"Sit, eat, and I'll fix it for you." She sets the freshly popped toast in front of Rylie and fetches condiments from the fridge. "What do you like on your toast?"

"Jam?"

Carriveau grabs two jars—one grape, the other strawberry—and leans over the table, pushing them in front of Rylie. In doing so, she gives the rapt teen another perfect view down her blouse.

"Would you like anything else?" She lingers there.

Rylie watches her breathe in, her lungs expanding, her breasts heaving in the push-up bra, her blouse pulled tight around them. She reaches slowly for the strawberry jam, averting her eyes from Carriveau's cleavage only when she realizes Miss Ansell has caught her being less than subtle about her interest in her Housemistress's breasts.

"*Non, merci beaucoup, Mademoiselle,*" she answers after a dazed pause.

"Very good." Carriveau straightens up.

Clang!

Thunk!

Upstairs, a girl shrieks, her cry of displeasure followed by laughter and shouting.

Carriveau and Miss Ansell share a look, each waiting for the other to respond. Since the noises appear to be emanating from the left side of the house, it seems reasonable to assume that the Upper Sixth girls are responsible for the ruckus.

"Two of your girls, *non*?" Carriveau urges Miss Ansell to go.

Once the slightly homely geography teacher has cleared the room, Carriveau moves around the table, positioning herself behind Rylie, trailing a hand lightly up the teen's arm and over her shoulder.

"You have such beautiful hair." She unravels the tangled braid. "Other women would kill for this." She digs her fingers in, dragging her manicured nails across Rylie's scalp.

Rylie offers a soft murmur of appreciation, relishing the feeling of Carriveau's long fingers running through her hair.

"Feels nice, *oui*?" Carriveau separates Rylie's hair into three equal chunks. "But perhaps you should try a ponytail tomorrow?" She manipulates Rylie's thick tresses gently but firmly. "I'm sure you can manage that?"

Rylie nods, unable to speak with her mouth full of toast.

"When you're done, please fix your uniform." Carriveau finishes off the braid. "You look like a ragamuffin, and I can't let you leave the house like that." She crosses to the other side of the room, pouring herself a cup of coffee from a freshly brewed pot.

"That's not a very nutritious breakfast," Rylie chides her, scoffing the last bite of toast. "Want me to make you something?"

Carriveau smiles wickedly, nursing her cup. "That would be an exception."

Rylie gets up to deposit her plate in the dishwasher, but before she can get past Carriveau, two

Lower Sixth girls burst into the kitchen, one chasing the other.

Barreling through the room without looking, the girl in front knocks into Rylie's back, shoving her forward and into Carriveau, in turn forcing Carriveau against the countertop.

More concerned about spilling her hot coffee all over Rylie than she is about the sudden invasion of her personal space, Carriveau lifts the cup up and directs it toward the sink.

When the second girl comes in hot pursuit of the first, she knocks the plate clean out of Rylie's hand.

It tumbles through the air.

Rylie lunges for it, but ...

Carriveau emits a reserved, involuntary 'oof' as their bodies collide, and the impact topples her sideways. Catching her before she loses her balance completely, Rylie makes a grab for anything she can get her hands around, resulting in another, stronger 'oof' when she makes contact with Carriveau's rear.

It lasts but a second, Rylie's hands hugging her tensed buttocks.

The plate smashes at their feet.

Carriveau jerks away, spinning to face the two unruly girls.

"*Arrêtez!*" she bellows, stopping them both instantly. "How dare you disrespect the rules of this house! No running!" She steps over the shattered plate. "Clean up this mess!"

She storms out of the room, and that's the last Rylie sees of her until it's time to depart for class. Rylie assumes she's hiding in her study, and doesn't expect her to come out until they've all left the house, so she's surprised to find her standing patiently by the front door when it's time for them to leave for morning registration and their first classes.

Fully prepared for this, the Upper and Lower Sixth girls line up in the hallway.

All but one, that is.

"What's going on?" Rylie whispers to Gabby.

"A kiss goodbye." Gabby blows her a smacker, grinning like a clown.

Confused, Rylie ends up at the back of the line and watches as Carriveau swings open the front door and proceeds to inspect the uniforms and appearances of all the girls before letting them leave the house, one at a time.

Upon passing inspection, she gives each a kiss on the forehead and sends them on their way. When she gets to Rylie, the last card in the deck, she's pleased to find that all earlier wardrobe malfunctions have been corrected. Ready to bid her goodbye, she leans in for the standard kiss ... but Rylie preempts her.

"Are you all right, Miss?"

"What? Since you molested me in the kitchen?" Carriveau chuckles. "I'll survive." She extends her hands in the motion of cupping Rylie's cheeks, but holds only the air. "Now, you pass muster, so do you want a kiss from me, or not? I do so only with your permission. You have every right to refuse."

Rylie dips her head, presenting her forehead for Carriveau's lips.

Like last night, the kiss is innocent and fleeting. Carriveau is about to pull away, but Rylie leans forward and draws her into a hug—or tries to. Carriveau seizes Rylie's arms before they manage to wrap all the way around her neck, and she brings the attempted closeness to an abrupt and premature end.

"Let's not get carried away." She keeps hold of Rylie's hands, kissing her fingers. "Think of me like a rainbow," she suggests. "Nice to look at, but always out of reach. *Tu comprends?*"

Suitably rebuffed, Rylie nods.

"*Merci, ma chère.*" Carriveau kisses her forehead again. "Off you go now. Don't be late for your first registration!"

She hurries Rylie out of the house, sending her to join Gabby, who's been waiting for her at the end of the small front garden. She waves the pair off, staying there by the door until Miss Ansell appears at her shoulder.

"Be careful with that one," she warns.

"She just needs to find her way here, that's all." Carriveau turns away, her smile dissolving, Miss Ansell's unwelcome advice stripping her good mood again. "She'll manage." The downcast Housemistress heads for her study. "As will I."

CHAPTER SIX

THE SCHOOL BELL SCREECHES THREE TIMES IN quick succession, heralding morning break. That's fifteen minutes between classes, in which time you can organize your notes for the next lesson, quickly grab a book from the library, or sneak a cigarette behind the indoor swimming pool at the south end of the campus.

"I owe you." Rylie crouches against the red brick wall, sucking on the first cigarette she's had in weeks. "I'll pay you back as soon as my parents send me my allowance."

"Nah, don't worry about it." Gabby taps ash onto the ground. "My brother sneaks me in two packs a week, and he's never asked for a penny. I reckon he's nicking 'em from somewhere."

"What else can he get?"

"What else do you want?"

Rylie shrugs. "How do you get booze around here?"

When Gabby laughs, she snorts smoke through her nostrils. "I like your thinking." She crushes the butt of her cigarette into the dirt. "Come on, let's go. I've got the mid-morning munchies."

Rylie takes one more puff, flicks the end of her cigarette into a bush, grabs her backpack off the ground, and follows Gabby back to the main school building. On the way, they cut through a small courtyard between the swimming pool and the covered tennis courts, passing a modern art sculpture at its center.

The imposing metal artwork is over eight feet high and comprised of two sets of three metal spirals. They start from narrow points at the top, gradually widening as they twirl toward the ground, and there are three distinct ribbons entwined in each set: gold, blue, and purple. A pair of white frilly knickers is dangling on the upper tip of one gold spiral.

"Oh, that's nice." Gabby squints up at the undies. "Very respectful."

Rylie studies the base of the sculpture, finding a dedication to Kaitlyn Simmons.

"Who's this Kaitlyn chick? And what makes her so special?" She brushes a fallen leaf off the plaque. "I've seen her picture in the house."

"She was a student here last year."

"A gymnast?" Rylie guesses, pinging one of the metal swirls. "Ribbon twirling?"

Gabby nods. "And lacrosse. All sports really."

"Where is she?"

"Gone, and you'd best not speak of her. Especially not to Miss Carriveau." Gabby grabs Rylie's hand, clasping her tightly. "Now foooooood!" She drags her new friend into the main school via a side door, their rubber-soled shoes slapping against the tiled floor.

Rounding a corner much too fast, they almost run headlong into Carriveau.

"Whoa!" Gabby skids to a halt, Rylie slamming into the back of her.

"*Ralentissez!*" Carriveau, laden with textbooks, orders them to slow down, one book slipping from her grasp. "*Faites attention, s'il vous plaît.*" She bends to retrieve the dropped text. "You girls are always in such a hurry."

Crouched before them, she glances up to flash the pair a stern glare, but her attention is snagged instead by their interlocked fingers, a bracelet peeking out from under the cuff of Rylie's cardigan. It's an elasticated band of wooden, rainbow-colored beads.

"Sorry, Miss!" Gabby starts backing away. "Sugar emergency!"

"Wait." Carriveau sets her books on a table of school pamphlets and calls them back.

She places a hand around each of their necks and tugs them forward, downward, and together, bringing their faces almost to her bosom as she leans over them, smelling their hair.

Busted.

She releases them, holding her hand out to Gabby, palm up. "Don't make me ask."

Gabby doesn't. She reaches into her backpack and hands over the cigarettes.

"*Merci.*" Carriveau picks up her books, sets the cigarettes on top of the pile, and holds the bundle to her chest, concealing the contraband. "That's the third time in as many weeks, Laurenson. You're getting sloppy."

"But I'm sixteen now," the teen grumps.

"But the school still forbids it. Now freshen up before class, *oui*?" She steps aside to let them pass. "You have me in"—she checks her watch—"four minutes."

"Yes, Miss." Gabby drags Rylie away.

"Walk, don't run," Carriveau scolds them again. "And do be careful." She fixes on their held hands. "You know how Missus Bursnell can be."

Rylie tries to apologize to Carriveau, but Gabby yanks her around another corner and Carriveau isn't looking anyway. They stop at a vending machine full of junk, and Gabby shoves enough money in to get a king-sized chocolate bar.

"Nom, nom, nom." She tears the wrapper open. "Elevenses!"

Rylie casts her eyes over the machine's offerings, nothing really sparking her interest until she spots a row of Skittles.

Taste the rainbow.

The candy's slogan leaps into the forefront of her mind and stays there, so she plugs in some coins, makes her choice, and a bag drops down into the tray. Delving in her backpack for more money, she inserts all the coins that she has and selects another bag.

And another.

And another.

And another, until she's drained the vending machine of Skittles.

"Jeepers! You've got a sweet tooth today, or what?" Gabby watches Rylie scoop them all out of the tray, struggling to hold them all.

"Yeah. Where can I get a bowl?"

Without any hesitation, Gabby strides over to the table of pamphlets, dumps out a bowlful of cheap, complimentary Larkhill fridge magnets, and passes the empty dish to Rylie.

"Whatchu up to? Who's this for?" She watches, bemused, as Rylie dumps the Skittles out of their packets and fills the bowl.

"*Mademoiselle Carriveau.*" Rylie digs in her backpack for a notepad and pen.

"Sucking up already?" Gabby snorts. "Why Skittles? Bit odd, ain't it? I believe tradition states that it's s'posed to be an apple, yeah?"

Rylie scribbles out a note. "It's sort of a private joke."

"How do you have a private joke with our house mum?" Gabby pulls a face. "You've been here less than twenty-four hours."

The bell rings for next class.

Rylie snatches up the bowl and lets Gabby lead the way to their English Language room, where she sets the offering down on Carriveau's desk, propping the note up in the middle of it.

"You're gonna get ribbed something chronic when other people find out about this." Gabby grabs her arm and leads her to a desk in the middle of the room. "They're gonna think you're kissing her arse."

"I'm not trying to win favor, I'm apologizing."

"What for this time?" Gabby shoves Rylie into the seat next to her. "Don't worry about the ciggies. She don't give a monkey's about that. She never reports anyone."

"It's not the smokes."

"What, then? Your mouth been running off with you again?"

"Something like that." Rylie organizes her books. "How can I tell if she likes me?"

"Did she tell you off?"

"No."

"Then she likes you." Gabby giggles, glancing over her shoulder at someone else in the class before lowering her voice. "Just watch you don't get Adel all ruffled up."

"What? Why?" Rylie cranks her neck to peer at Adel in the corner. "What's it to her?"

"She's Miss Carriveau's little pet."

With the clatter of pencil cases and the crinkle of notepaper dying down, Carriveau breezes into the room, making a beeline for her desk. Upon her entrance, the children stand respectfully, waiting to receive the command to sit.

That command is somewhat late in coming, however, as Carriveau reaches her desk and catches sight of the colorful bowl of candy. She sits, plucking the note from within it.

On one side, there's a simple apology: *Je suis désolée, mais ...*

She flips it over.

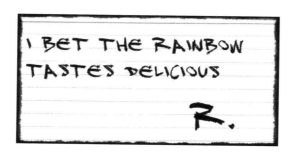

As much as she tries, she can't fight the smile completely. Nor can she hide the blush on her cheeks, which only intensifies when she looks up and finds Rylie beaming at her.

Incapable of ignoring her hunger for sex, her cunt pulsing beneath her desk, it takes several seconds for her to compose herself enough to clear her throat and bark out the word "Sit."

While the children settle themselves into their chairs, she crosses her legs, clenching her thighs together, trying not to think about how wet she is. Still flushed, she grabs a wad of papers off her desk and fans herself, making a token complaint about the temperature of the room.

Enthralled by this display, Gabby angles herself toward Rylie and whispers in her ear. "What the shit did you write in that note?!"

Of course, Rylie doesn't tender an answer. Her own anatomy begins to throb as Carriveau's eyes meet hers again, and her heart swells to bursting when Carriveau puts the note to one side. She doesn't throw it in the trash, or hide it away in a drawer, she leans it against a stack of textbooks directly in front of her.

Further appreciation comes unexpectedly when, during a silent period of independent study, Carriveau gets up from her desk and weaves her way through the rows of students, peering over their shoulders to check on the progress of their work.

At Rylie's desk, without adjusting her pace, she trails her hand over Rylie's shoulders, from right to left. It begins much the same as their light contact had at breakfast, with her hand making its way up to Rylie's right shoulder, but this time, she doesn't stop. She gives a gentle squeeze, then tickles her fingertips over Rylie's neck, beginning just below one ear and finishing below the other. From there, she slides her hand down Rylie's left arm, then drifts away, moving on to another desk, clasping both hands behind her back.

This small, sensual gesture makes Rylie gasp and shiver, and while it goes unnoticed by most of the class, there's one particularly attentive girl who witnesses the entire demonstration: Adel Edwards.

Following a rather unimpressive dinner of vegetarian lasagna in the refectory, Rylie joins Gabby in the house study room for a mandatory hour of silent homework, then the pair retreats to the kitchen for a bowl of ice cream. Other sixth formers are milling about the house, watching television, some still doing their homework, listening to music in the dormitories, or reading.

Done marking Year Nine coursework, Miss Ansell swoops into the common room and takes charge of the television remote, thus preventing the outbreak of war for its possession, but causing an exodus of discontented Upper and Lower Sixth girls to flood the halls when she changes the channel to a marathon of Meerkat Manor.

In the wake of this disruption, Carriveau—now also done with her evening paperwork—has a hard time tracking down the newest addition to her house.

"Oh, there you are!" She pokes her head around the kitchen doorway, finding Rylie and Gabby slathering their ice cream in chocolate sauce. "I've been looking for you."

The two teens start to rise from their chairs, but Carriveau gestures for them to remain seated.

"No, no," she insists. "I don't want to interrupt, but Harcourt, I'd like to see you in my study when you're finished." Her eyes flit to Gabby, then back to Rylie. "Take your time."

She's gone in a flash, and Rylie's left wondering what more she could possibly have done wrong. Gobbling up her ice cream as fast as her body will allow, she cleans herself up and knocks on Carriveau's study door less than ten minutes later.

"*Entrez!*" is the welcoming response.

Somewhat shyly, Rylie opens the door and steps inside, finding Carriveau seated behind her desk. With her hair pinned back and her reading glasses on, she looks bookish and conservative, but that changes quite dramatically when she sets her glasses aside and stands up.

She's shed her jacket, her blouse clinging to every curve. It's tight around her bust, the lacy imprint of her bra showing through, hinting at the presence of two slightly erect nipples.

This woman is not bookish nor conservative.

She's a vixen.

"I spoke to Missus Bursnell about changing your enrollments," she says, leaning on the front of her desk, waiting for Rylie to close the door before she continues.

"It's bad news?" Rylie assumes, sealing their privacy. "She said no?"

"Not quite." Carriveau invites Rylie over to the leather sofa. "I've been instructed to test your proficiency before I'm allowed to accept you into my class." She sits on the far end of the sofa, swiveled to face her pupil, leaving a cautious distance between them. "I thought the best way to do this might be"—she hesitates for emphasis—"orally."

Taste the rainbow.

Rylie can't help it. That slogan springs back into her head at full force, and to make matters worse, the bowl of Skittles has been placed prominently in the center of the coffee table.

This is tit for tat, she thinks, her cheeks on fire. She'd made Carriveau blush in class, and now this is some kind of private payback.

"Wh ... I sh ..." She tries to keep her mind away from oral sex. "I ... this is ... gah." She blows air through her lips and rests her hands on her knees, determined not to fidget.

Seeing her discomfort, Carriveau laughs and eases up. "Tongue-tied?" She kicks off her shoes. "Not a good way to begin."

"What do you, umm, want me to speak about?" Rylie recovers herself somewhat.

"Anything, as long as you say it *en français.*" Carriveau tucks her feet beneath herself, causing her skirt to ride up a few more inches. "Tell me about Rylie Harcourt."

Over the course of the next hour and beyond, they converse in French. Rylie makes Carriveau laugh, not only with her stories, but also by butchering the odd word here and there, mixing up her prepositions, and stumbling over some of the more complex sentence structures. All in all, though, she demonstrates more than enough aptitude to warrant being included in Carriveau's class, and the conversation flows so easily between them that the true objective of this *tête-a-tête* is very nearly forgotten altogether. Indeed, it's not until Carriveau finds herself stifling a yawn that she thinks to check the time.

"Goodness! It's been almost two hours!" She looks twice at her watch, just to be sure it hasn't stopped. "It's nearly curfew!"

"Well, how did I do?" Rylie smiles sheepishly. "Am I good enough for you? Do you want me?"

Carriveau ignores the blindingly obvious *double sens* in both of those questions.

"*Ton français est très bon.*" She praises Rylie's linguistic prowess, telling her how good her French is. "Perhaps you have no need of any private tutelage after all," she threatens. "You already seem to have a firm grasp of things."

Rylie's mind flashes back to the kitchen, cupping Carriveau's tight *derrière* with both hands, wishing she'd had the nerve to squeeze.

On that note, "My grasp could be firmer."

Continuing to ignore the lines being fed to her, even though she's guilty of setting Rylie up for them, Carriveau keeps the focus on language.

71

"I confess, I've enjoyed hearing you speak French. So seldom do I hear my first tongue outside of the classroom. Much less spoken well." She holds Rylie's gaze. "*Tu me fais frémir, ma chère.*"

Pouncing on the thinly veiled confession that Carriveau quivers in her presence—veiled in part by way of it being spoken in French instead of English, and partly by slipping it in alongside a legitimate appreciation for linguistic proficiency—Rylie feels brave enough to offer up an admission of her own.

"*Tu es très gentille, Mademoiselle Carriveau.*" She's riveted by her Housemistress's plump red lips. "*Quand je suis près de toi, je me sens—*"

You're very nice, Miss Carriveau.

When I'm close to you, I feel—

Fearful of where that sentence might be going, Carriveau doesn't let her get any further.

"Oh, my sweet girl." She scooches forward and presses her palm to Rylie's cheek. "I'm afraid that you might've found a way into my affections already." She drops her hand to Rylie's lap, patting her thigh. "But we really must call it a night."

She slips on her shoes and gets up from the sofa without allowing Rylie any chance to respond, then prepares to show her eager pupil to the door. But although Rylie follows her off the sofa, the hesitant teen doesn't take any steps forward.

"Is there something wrong?" Carriveau doubles back.

Now seems like as good a time as any to bring up one niggling issue that's been gnawing at her since last night's failed flirtation in her cubicle, so Rylie just spits it out.

"*Putain* means whore." She looks away, scratching at an ink stain on her new cardigan. "You said it when you were helping me with my bed, and I know I gave the wrong impression when I stuck my arse out at you like a baboon in heat, but I don't want you to think that I'm—"

"I didn't call you a whore." Carriveau stops her from digging herself into a hole. "That's one fairly literal translation of the word, but it's used primarily as an exclamation in France." She lowers her voice almost to a whisper, as if afraid that someone else might hear. "Like 'fuck', you understand? It wasn't meant as an insult, only an exclamation of my surprise."

"Oh." Rylie works that over in her mind, feeling daft for having fixated on it.

"But still"—Carriveau takes Rylie by the chin and forces her to look up—"I shouldn't have said it. To do so was terribly unprofessional. Please forgive me."

Forgiveness comes in a second.

An embrace follows.

Rylie slides her arms around Carriveau's neck— as she'd tried to do that very morning—and sinks into the French woman's warm breast with a desperate sigh of longing.

Too shocked to respond appropriately, Carriveau stands rigid, a sharp intake of breath trapped in her lungs. She hasn't the nerve to reciprocate, nor the desire to push the child away.

"*Qu'est-ce que tu fais?*" she whispers, reaching tentatively for Rylie's waist. "What are you doing?" She translates herself needlessly, knowing that Rylie understands perfectly well. "This isn't allowed." Her hands traverse the contours of the young girl's body, sweeping around her back, one hand remaining there while the other glides upward to caress her shoulders.

More telling than her words, Carriveau doesn't force the embrace to end.

"This isn't allowed," she whispers again, her cheek pressed to Rylie's hair.

Emboldened by the lack of a rebuke, Rylie nuzzles her face into the hollow of Carriveau's neck, inhaling the scent of her perfume.

"You're so beautiful," she murmurs, her lips brushing Carriveau's collar bone before closing over it, laying a single velvet kiss there.

As perhaps was the intention, the flustered Housemistress is so focused on the actions of Rylie's mouth, the teen's breath hot against her skin, she doesn't at first realize that one of Rylie's arms is slipping slowly from her shoulder, a daring hand sliding brazenly toward her breast.

But when she does …

"*Ça suffit*! That's enough!" She captures the wandering hand, swiftly separating herself from her venturesome new pupil. "You ought to get ready for bed now. We've been far too long in each other's company." She marches Rylie to the door. "Bed check in five minutes."

Rylie stands alone in the hallway for a few moments before ascending the stairs. Not sure whether to conclude that her private time with Carriveau ended on a positive note or a negative one, she simply brushes her teeth and goes straight to bed.

From her cubicle, she can see two girls—the same pair as the night before—fooling around, squished into one tiny bed. They're kissing, giggling, and whimpering, one girl's hand up the other's nightdress.

"Boo!" Gabby thrusts her head over the dividing wall to Rylie's immediate left, flashing a toothy grin. "What did our old mum want with ya? You was in there for ages!"

Rylie shrugs. "Just some stuff about my class enrollments." She tips her head to the canoodling pair. "Aren't they worried Miss Carriveau will catch them doing that?"

"Pfft!" Gabby blows a raspberry. "They like to tease her. But if you ask me, I think it's cruel."

"Cruel?" Rylie lays her pajamas out on her bed. "Why?"

"After what happened with Kaitlyn? Shit, I'm surprised Miss Carriveau can still bear to look at us, never mind be as kind as she is. I reckon I'd wanna run a hundred miles if I was her."

Before Rylie can press her to expound on that, the dormitory door opens and Carriveau—her jacket back on and buttoned up—announces her arrival for bed checks.

Seemingly in a rush to get this chore over and done with, she walks briskly down the aisle, hurrying through her goodnights with the odd "Pick that up," or "You'll need to clean that in the morning" thrown in for good measure.

When she gets to one conspicuously empty cubicle, she plants her hands on her hips and calls out the girl's name, drawing the horny teen away from her would-be bedmate.

"Say goodnight and get back to your own cubicle, Richardson."

The girl does as instructed, giving her lover a long parting kiss, tongues and all, and Carriveau keeps her eyes on them from beginning to end, exploiting her peripheral vision to steal a perfect view of Rylie, topless as she changes into her pajamas.

When Richardson finally slips back into her own cubicle, Carriveau whips her bum with a discarded towel she picks off the floor.

Richardson squeals. "Would you like one of my goodnight kisses, too, Miss?"

For one shocking second, Rylie thinks she just might. Carriveau slings the towel over the cubicle wall, grabs Richardson's chin, and tilts her head up.

"Watch your mouth, you cheeky girl." A smile twitches at the corners of her lips and she releases the sassy teen, resuming her nightly arc of the dorm.

At Rylie's cubicle, she slips a hand inside one of her jacket pockets and fishes out something small, concealing it in her palm.

"So how was your first day?" she asks, stepping as close to the thin yellow line as she dares. "It's a lot to adapt to, I'm sure." She takes Rylie's hand in hers, mimicking a reassuring touch. "It'll take some time to get used to the boundaries we all must stick to."

Rylie feels a slip of paper press into her palm, and she holds it there with her thumb as Carriveau withdraws, giving nothing away.

Her heart pounding impatiently, she waits for Carriveau to complete the bed checks and turn out the lights before she dives for her bed. Even then, she waits until the room falls silent—the echo of Carriveau's stiletto heels departing—before she slides her cell phone out from underneath her pillow and uses its glow to read the secret bedtime note.

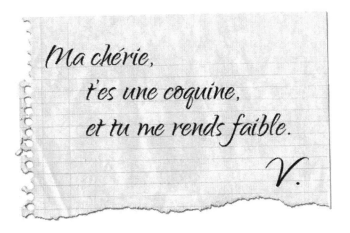

Ma chérie,

t'es une coquine,

et tu me rends faible.

V.

My darling,
You're a tease, and you make me weak.

Lying there, holding the note to her chest, Rylie stares up at the ceiling, aware of a distinct heat between her thighs. It's been days since she's had the opportunity to tend to certain physical needs, and until this moment, it hadn't occurred to her how having to share a dorm with eleven other people might negatively impact her ability to sate her passions.

She considers sneaking into the bathroom for a quick rub, but she can't be bothered to get up. She also considers setting her alarm twenty minutes earlier than usual, and slipping into the bathroom before anyone else is awake, but she knows she'll hate that idea when morning comes. Instead, she decides to do as Adel had done last night: wait until everyone else is likely to be asleep, then get down to business.

Playing solitaire on her phone—even though the use of electronics is forbidden after lights out—she lets twenty minutes tick by.

Twenty-one.

Twenty-two.

As she hits the half an hour mark, the anticipation of an orgasm has her absolutely gushing and she can't hold off any longer. Setting her phone down, she drives her hand under the covers, inside her pajama bottoms, and between her legs. Unfortunately, as she smothers a deep gasp of need, someone else in the room lets one out.

Rylie freezes. Could it be? Again? Adel?

"Oh, Vivienne, fuck me ..."

Yup.

Scowling, Rylie pulls her hand out of her pajamas, gets up on her knees, and prepares to chuck a stuffed animal at Adel's head, but once she's high enough to look over the cubicle wall, her eyes are drawn immediately to the door.

The shadows are there, just like last night. Carriveau! Did she return out of curiosity? Hope for a repeat performance? Sheer coincidence? Whatever the reason for her reappearance, tonight, she leaves before Adel reaches her peak.

CHAPTER SEVEN

Two weeks pass. Every evening, flirtatious glances are exchanged across the refectory. Carriveau always seems to pick a seat with a direct eyeline across the room, and Rylie chooses to believe that she's doing so on purpose. Back at the house, Carriveau continues to invite Rylie into her study for private tutoring, which begins as something mildly unnecessary and becomes gradually more pointless as time goes on.

They converse in French, for the most part, but Carriveau's syllabus notes go from her lap to the coffee table, and then never leave her desk. The ratio of English to French starts to increase, and there's a great deal of laughter. Carriveau talks about herself at least as much as Rylie does, and their conversation moves from the sofa to the floor as the wayward bound Housemistress starts pulling out photo albums to illustrate her stories.

"I grew up in *Provence*." She shows Rylie pictures of *la Côte d'Azur*. "But I feel as British as the gloomy weather," she jokes. "I've lived here since I was sixteen. I'm thirty-one now, so that's almost half my life."

"I still can't believe you speak seven languages." Rylie shuffles a few inches closer to better see the album, their backs leaning against the bookshelf, their shoes castoff by the desk. "I can barely wrap my brain around two."

"Seven fluently," Carriveau corrects her. "I speak several more in bits and pieces."

"Bragger." Rylie flips the page.

In the next set of pictures, Carriveau is with another female. The two appear close, often photographed holding hands or embracing. In one photo, they're kissing.

"Girlfriend?" Rylie enquires, keeping her tone neutral, hoping the question conveys merely a casual interest.

"Ex."

"You're gay?"

"You're nosy." Carriveau snaps the album shut, playfully trying to trap her fingers.

"I'm curious," Rylie defends herself. "Are you not out on campus? Is that why you won't say?"

"No-one's 'out' on this campus," Carriveau reminds her sadly. "So be discreet."

"With what?"

"Gabby Laurenson. I can see that the pair of you have become quite close in the last fortnight." The smile that'd been so firmly pinned on Carriveau's lips falls away. "You can rest assured that you shan't ever be chastised for anything the two of you do in this house, but elsewhere, you must play by Missus Bursnell's rules."

Rylie shakes her head. "I don't fancy Gabby." She twists sideways to look at Carriveau. "But I *am* gay, if that's what you're wondering. If that was your way of asking."

"It wasn't." Carriveau pings the rainbow bead bracelet on Rylie's wrist.

"That doesn't necessarily mean I'm gay." Rylie strokes the back of her hand down Carriveau's arm. "It just means I like rainbows."

Carriveau suppresses a shiver and diverts her attention to the closed album in her lap, picking at a dented corner. "Why would you be interested in something you can never get your hands on?"

"Chasing it's half the fun." Rylie lifts the album out of Carriveau's lap, pushing the distraction away. "Besides, the rainbow wants to be chased."

"*Ah bon*? Is that so?" Carriveau turns her head, emerald eyes fixing on blue.

"Uh-huh. Nothing that beautiful likes to be ignored." Rylie edges closer. "Plus, if it didn't like the attention, it wouldn't flaunt itself."

She pinches the open collar of Carriveau's blouse between her fingers, easing the fabric aside, baring more of her Housemistress's generous breasts, looking but not touching.

"Rylie ..." Breathing heavily, Carriveau remains motionless. "Please ..."

Not sure if that's meant as a supplication or a warning, Rylie hedges her bets and drops her hand to Carriveau's lap, seeking out the French woman's fingers, creeping her own over top.

"Don't do this." Carriveau slips her hand away. "Don't tempt me. Can't you see how much I'm already struggling? How much I want—" She stops herself from completing the confession and turns her head, both to break the magnetism and to hide her watery eyes. "I'm afraid that's it for tonight. It's bedtime."

"All right." After two weeks of this same routine, Rylie knows better than to argue. "I'll see you upstairs in a few minutes." She picks herself up off the floor and retrieves her shoes, leaving silently.

Ironing appears to be a skill that one must acquire through practice, Rylie concludes, growling with frustration at a shirt that refuses to relinquish its creases. She's been in the laundry room wrestling with the uncooperative garment for far too long, and her patience is wearing thin.

Last night's session with Carriveau ended on a high note that stuck with her till morning, right up until she received a dress code warning from Missus Bursnell, who told her she looked like a tatterdemalion and ought to sharpen herself up before she winds up in detention.

Brilliant.

She'd run out of clean shirts several days ago, was forced to do a wash, and thought she could get away with hanging them to dry, figuring that the wrinkles would fall out of them.

Apparently not.

She lays the buttoned up shirt out over the ironing board again and drags the iron from collar to hem, catching on every button on the way down.

"Motherfu—" She catches the curse word in her throat as Carriveau appears in the doorway. "Oh, shit," she says instead, looking at her watch. "Am I late for our ... thing?"

Carriveau closes the door and leans against it, rapping her fingers on the wood, thinking deeply before she speaks. "It's time for our private lessons to end."

"Oh." Rylie looks crestfallen. "Why?"

"I think you can imagine why." Carriveau takes a step closer, then hesitates, appearing to contemplate something before coming to a decision that announces itself with a heavy sigh of resignation. "You've never ironed before, have you?"

Rylie shakes her head. "I'm not even sure my mother has." She makes another halfhearted effort with the iron, but achieves nothing.

Without explanation, Carriveau strips off her jacket, flings it over a washing machine, and crosses the room, moving behind Rylie and out of sight, her stilettos clicking rhythmically on the floor tiles.

Then, the clicking stops.

Silence.

Rylie is about to turn and ask for help when, suddenly, she's encased in warmth. Carriveau is at her back, against her, close enough to transfer body heat between them, moving slowly and precisely.

"I can't bear to watch you. It's too painful." She reaches around Rylie's waist, sets the iron aside, and takes the shirt in her hands. "Like standing by while you struggled to make your bed on your first night." Her voice is like caramel, sweet and soft, her breath like fire against Rylie's neck as she leans forward to tease the shirt open. "It's a torture to see you like that." She unfastens one button at a time, as if undressing a lover, her breasts pushed up against Rylie's shoulder blades, her lips grazing the young teen's ear. *"Tu comprends, ma minette?"*

Rylie nods, understanding the *double sens* perfectly: Miss Carriveau wants her!

She feels blood rushing between her legs, responding to Carriveau's daring use of a highly inappropriate endearment: my pussycat. Reacting instinctively, she tilts her head, baring her neck, offering her peachy skin to Carriveau for kisses, should she feel inclined to give them. Unfortunately, she doesn't.

"You're going about this all wrong." Carriveau nuzzles her cheek against Rylie's head, clinging to the ruse the shirt provides as she drapes it over the ironing board. "Let me show you."

She flattens one half of the shirt out, starting with the buttoned edge, and nudges Rylie to retrieve the iron from its cradle.

"You start like this," she explains, placing a hand over Rylie's on the iron. "And you have to go slowly." She guides Rylie over the fabric. "Don't force it." The iron sizzles against the cotton. "Don't rush." She weaves the tip of the iron in between the buttons. "Please, don't rush. You have to give the heat time to build." She bears down slightly on Rylie's hand. "Now apply a little more pressure."

"Like this?" Rylie presses harder on the iron, simultaneously arching her back, pushing her rear into Carriveau's crotch.

"Mm-hmm." Carriveau brings a hand to Rylie's hip, resting it there. *"Tu fais cela très bien. J'aime ça."*

Rylie's breasts tingle beneath her uniform, her nipples swelling and stiffening with arousal. She knows full well that Carriveau is exploiting her mother tongue to convey that which cannot be so easily concealed in *double sens*, nor spoken freely.

By offering up these compliments and endearments in French, Carriveau leaves her words open to interpretation. In this case, what could be completely genuine praise of Rylie's ironing—you're doing that very well—almost legitimizes the subsequent, more obvious appreciation of the action of her *derrière*: I like that.

Almost, but not quite.

Capitalizing on the back-and-forth movement of the ironing—doing her bit to maintain the subterfuge—Rylie keeps in constant motion, repeatedly bumping her backside into Carriveau.

This goes on for a minute or two, progress being made slowly on the shirt, then Carriveau withdraws her hand from the iron.

An audible suspiration of disappointment immediately leaves Rylie's lips, her confidence faintly shaken. Has Carriveau had enough? Is she bored? Not even a little.

"Keep going," the French woman insists, reading Rylie's mind and transferring her free hand to the teen's other hip. *"S'il te plaît."*

Far from being bored, she's now using both hands to more actively direct the intensity of the contact between them. Delighted by that, Rylie pushes back harder, practically grinding herself into her Housemistress. In response, Carriveau tightens her grip, the friction between them increasing as she rocks her own pelvis forward, subtly and gently causing Rylie's thrusts to hit home even more firmly.

At this point, Rylie drops the subterfuge. She whines, abandons the iron, and wiggles her bum shamelessly against Carriveau's crotch. For her part, Carriveau brings one hand up, under Rylie's skirt, gripping her bare inner thigh, admitting quietly:

"*Je n'arrête pas de penser à toi.*"

I can't stop thinking about you.

Rylie whimpers, pushing back harder, yearning to feel Carriveau's fingers inside her.

But she's denied.

Carriveau drags her fingernails over Rylie's tender flesh, her thumb scarcely an inch away from the teen's hot, wet sex. She refrains from venturing any further, but Rylie's arousal is so heightened that she doesn't even need direct contact.

A small orgasm ripples through her, and she clutches the edge of the ironing board to hold herself up, a low moan escaping from her lips, muffled against the crumpled up shirt.

When the shivers subside and her body goes limp, Carriveau leans over her arched back and rescues the shirt, setting the iron back down on its cradle.

"Are you done?"

Rylie manages a nod and an affirmative squeak.

"All right, then." Carriveau peels away from her. "I think it's time for bed."

Rylie practically collapses on the ironing board, groaning discontentedly.

"Ah, the urgency of youth," Carriveau teases her. "Always so impatient."

"But ... my shirt ..." Rylie protests weakly.

"No buts, *ma chérie.*" Carriveau spanks her bum and sends her out of the room. "Go on and get yourself ready for bed."

Halfway across the room, Rylie looks back over her shoulder, finding Carriveau about to finish the ironing of the shirt herself.

"Miss, you don't have to—"

"Go," Carriveau urges, waving her off. "Don't be late up to the dorm."

Rylie starts to do as she's told, but turns back again in the doorway. "You'll come say goodnight, won't you?"

"*Bien sûr.*" Carriveau beams. "Of course."

Slightly shaky and lightheaded, her cunt still in spasms, Rylie makes her way upstairs to the Lower Sixth dormitory. In a daze, she pulls on her pajamas, brushes her teeth, washes her face, and drags a brush through her hair, unable to think of anything but the lingering sensation of Carriveau's hand on her thigh, the scratches on her skin a visible reminder of her Housemistress's nails digging into her, making her come instantly.

Indeed, Carriveau's mere presence is enough to arouse her. One look at her red lips, her proud cleavage, or her shapely rear, and she gets flooded— even more so tonight. When Carriveau arrives at the dormitory for bed checks—carrying with her a pristinely ironed shirt—Rylie's nipples stiffen and jut out, showing through her thin cotton pajamas.

As her turn to be wished goodnight rolls around, she stands up straight, her shoulders back, making sure her assets are on display.

"I think you left this in the laundry room." Carriveau hands over the shirt, refusing to let her eyes wander. "Hang it up right away, else it'll crease again."

"*Oui, merci beaucoup.*"

After the exchange of the shirt and a smile, Rylie retreats to the back of her cubicle and slips the still warm garment onto a hanger. As she straightens the starchy cotton, her fingers come into contact with something pinned to the inside, just below the last buttonhole.

It's a note, written in Occitan.

On the back, she finds the English translation: For nothing is as hard to gain as that which I am seeking, nor any longing affects me as that for what I cannot have.

Rylie's eyes dart up, following Carriveau as she completes her circuit of the dorm.

"Goodnight, Edwards." The Housemistress sighs, keeping well clear of the thin yellow line. "I'm very tired tonight."

At the door, she flashes Rylie a fleeting smile, turns out the lights, and vanishes into the darkness, the now familiar sound of her retreating footsteps echoing down the empty hallway.

Too wired to sleep, Rylie grabs her phone, curls up under her duvet, and texts back and forth with old friends, catching up on recent gossip from her former school. Without meaning to, she kills an hour and most of her battery, and it's not until she finally rolls over to go to sleep that she realizes the dormitory has been awfully quiet tonight.

Adel hasn't partaken in any nocturnal pleasures, which, up till this point, have occurred nightly and like clockwork. Perhaps she's tired, Rylie thinks, letting out a yawn of her own.

Tired.

Like Miss Carriveau.

That's an intriguing thought, and Rylie fleshes it out further. What if it was no accident that Carriveau was standing outside the dormitory door on that first night? What if her return the following evening was equally contrived? Has she been standing out there every night? Rylie hadn't thought to check. Could Adel's midnight wanking sessions be deliberately staged for Carriveau's pleasure?

Rylie falls asleep with her hand inside her knickers, teasing her drenched sex.

CHAPTER EIGHT

Carriveau moans into her pillow, her chestnut hair flopping over her face and shoulders as she sinks limply into the sheets, her third orgasm of the morning ebbing away.

"*Je n'en reviens pas,*" she pants, rolling onto her back, astounded by the intensity of her climax, finally feeling somewhat sated.

Flooded with endorphins, she shuts off her alarm before it has a chance to shrill at her, then gets herself ready for work in record time. Rushing through morning paperwork in her study, she's still feeling the buzz of sexual euphoria when she bursts into the Lower Sixth dormitory at seven o'clock on the dot.

"*Réveillez-vous!*" She claps her hands together, beaming broadly. "It's a brand new day!"

Swooping through the room, she makes sure every girl is at least partially conscious and in the process of rising from bed, then turns to Rylie's cubicle.

Rylie's *empty* cubicle.

The bed's made, the pressed shirt's gone, and there's no sign of the teen.

Carriveau feels a small flutter of panic, and she grabs Gabby's elbow as the groggy redhead stumbles out of the adjoining cubicle.

"*Où est Harcourt?*" she demands. "Where's Rylie?"

"Huh?" Gabby rubs sleep out of her eyes, squinting at Rylie's bed. "I dunno."

Giving the dorm another once over, satisfied that Rylie hasn't risen from another girl's bed instead of her own, Carriveau hurries from the room and down the stairs, brushing past Miss Ansell without so much as a flicker of acknowledgment.

"Trouble at mill?" the confused geography teacher calls after her, but even that goes ignored.

Carriveau continues her search for Rylie on the ground floor, starting with the study room, then the common room, then the kitchen.

"*Dieu merci!*" She presses a hand to her chest, very much relieved to find Rylie making breakfast. "I didn't know where you were. Why are you up so early?"

Rylie drops two slices of bread in the nearest toaster. "I thought if I got up early enough then you might be able to show me how to use this strange toasting contraption." She leans forward, shaking her bum in Carriveau's direction.

Smiling wryly, all worry evaporated, Carriveau walks slowly toward her. "I think I can help with that." She pushes the lever on the toaster. "*Voilà!*"

"Boo." Rylie feigns a sulk.

"Perhaps you'd like to wish me good morning?" Carriveau offers instead. "*En français*, of course."

Knowing that a greeting *en français* means *faire la bise*—a kiss on each cheek—Rylie very carefully invades Carriveau's personal space, first planting a delicate peck on the right cheek, then the left, taking her time with both.

"*Bonjour, Mademoiselle Carriveau,*" she coos softly, slipping a hand onto her Housemistress's slender waist.

"Careful." Carriveau peels that opportunistic hand away, kissing Rylie's fingers. "Please be careful." She kisses the teen's palm. "You have to control these wandering hands of yours."

"But not my lips?"

Carriveau shrugs. "I'm French. A kiss or two on the cheek is like a handshake, *n'est-ce pas*? It's perfectly harmless."

"So another won't hurt? Just lips, no hands."

Carriveau doesn't voice an objection, so Rylie leans forward and presses her mouth firmly to the French woman's cheek, letting the peck linger a fraction of a second longer than could be considered platonic.

"I really like you," she whispers, her lips to Carriveau's ear.

"I'd noticed," Carriveau whispers back, placing her hands upon Rylie's shoulders, ready to push her away if she should grow bold enough to make another advance.

Feeling the tension in her Housemistress's touch, Rylie pulls back of her own accord—albeit only a few inches. Her eyes are drawn to Carriveau's mouth, those glossy red lips of hers slightly parted and so tantalizingly inviting.

Rylie encroaches again. "Just lips, no hands," she repeats, tilting her head and moving in for a full-on lip-lock.

"Don't." Carriveau gasps as Rylie's bottom lip bumps hers. "Please don't."

"Why not?" Rylie stays put, rubbing their noses together. "Last night—"

Carriveau puts a finger to the teen's lips, silencing her and moving her back. "Last night was a reckless indulgence." She keeps her finger where it is, tracing Rylie's lower lip with the tip. "I'm not your peer, and this attraction between us is no trivial thing."

Rylie closes her hot mouth around Carriveau's fingertip, gently kissing it.

"I won't ignore it—I *can't* ignore it—but we mustn't ... this shouldn't ..." Halfway through that thought, Carriveau loses the ability to speak.

She becomes entranced by the action of Rylie's mouth as the teen's lips part and she flicks her tongue around the digit before kissing it again, sucking it deeper than before. But it's over in seconds.

Something in Carriveau's voice—a note of desperation perhaps—triggers Rylie to recall a conversation she'd had with Gabby when she first arrived at Larkhill. Just before bed check, Gabby said she was surprised that Carriveau could still bear to look at them "After what happened with Kaitlyn."

Well, what *did* happen with Kaitlyn? Rylie never followed up. Did Kaitlyn break Carriveau's heart? If that's the case, surely all she needs is a bit of reassurance …

Rylie pulls Carriveau's finger out of her mouth with a pop. "I've wanted to kiss you since the first time I saw you, before I even knew who you were." She places both hands on Carriveau's waist, drawing her reluctant Housemistress closer. "There was never any doubt."

She leans in for the smooch, lips grazing lips, Carriveau neither encouraging nor blocking her advance, but then …

Footsteps.

Chatter.

Hungry sixth formers are descending for breakfast, and Carriveau withdraws. Much too late to do anything about it—to offer comfort or concern— Rylie notices tears in her beautiful Housemistress's eyes. Did she cause that? Are the tears for her? Or Kaitlyn? Or something else entirely? What just happened?

Carriveau makes a hasty retreat to her study, leaving Rylie confused and conflicted, worried that she's locked herself away to cry. Fortunately, when she emerges at the last minute for her routine uniform inspections and kisses goodbye, she looks perfectly composed.

Rylie ends up at the back of the line again, but on purpose this time. Ever hopeful that Carriveau might give her a little something extra, she likes to be the last one out of the house. Not that she's ever received anything more than the standard peck on the forehead, mind you, and this morning proves to be no exception.

She receives her usual goodbye and leaves without fuss, but halfway down the garden path, she decides to take matters into her own hands. Marching back to the house, she follows Carriveau into her study and finds her standing in front of her desk, gathering up test papers.

The thud of a backpack hitting the floor alerts Carriveau to Rylie's presence, but leaves her little time to react to it.

"I'm sorry," Rylie offers in advance.

"*Pour quoi faire?*" Carriveau looks shocked. "What for?"

"This." Rylie lunges at her, kissing her on the lips before she knows it's coming.

The closed-mouth kiss is so forceful that Carriveau is shoved back against her desk, almost knocked completely off her feet, test papers scattering to the floor. She brings a hand up to push Rylie back, but by the time she makes contact with her overly enthusiastic suitor, she's lost all inclination to do so.

"I know what I want." Rylie breaks the kiss and holds her unsteady Housemistress upright. "*J'ai envie de toi, Mademoiselle Carriveau.*" She tenders another quick peck, keeping her hands in place until she's sure Carriveau can keep herself on her feet. "I want *you.*"

Following that confident proclamation, she spins on her heels, grabs her backpack off the floor, and exits the house, leaving Carriveau struck dumb.

When Miss Ansell passes by Carriveau's study a few minutes later, not much has changed. Carriveau is still propped against her desk, breathing erratically, test papers strewn about her feet.

"Are you feeling okay?" Miss Ansell raises a questioning eyebrow.

Carriveau snaps herself out of her stupor. "*Oui.*"

"What happened?"

"I ..." Carriveau gets down on her knees, collecting her papers. "I felt dizzy for a moment, that's all. *Ce n'est pas grave.*" She waves the incident off as nothing serious.

"Are you sick?"

"Maybe." Carriveau takes a deep breath, fearful of her emotions spilling out all over the place. "In one way or another."

Carriveau strides into her Year Twelve French classroom with no hint of a smile, lesson notes and homework cradled in one arm.

"*Asseyez-vous,*" she orders them to sit, snapping her fingers to urge speed as she dumps her books and papers onto her desk with a loud smack.

She's in a bad mood, that much is obvious. For the next sixty minutes, she barks out instructions and reprimands, picking on every minor fault, offering few pleasantries and little encouragement. She refuses to make eye contact with Rylie, even when Rylie puts up her hand with a genuine answer to a question, and her interactions with the other students are noticeably more brusque than usual.

After a while, Rylie gives up, her own demeanor turning sour. By the time the bell rings, she's in a downright miserable mood and is keen to get out of the classroom, keeping her eyes to herself as she walks past Carriveau's desk on her way to the door.

It's lunchtime, but since she's neither inclined to be sociable in the refectory, nor run the risk of bumping into Carriveau at the house, she opts to mope. For the most part, that means wandering aimlessly around school property, discovering new places where one could hide and smoke, and mapping out more shortcuts to and from her classes.

Along the way, she finds a room that wasn't included in the grand tour Souliere had taken her on when she first arrived. Normally completely locked off, the main doors to this enormous room are plastered with 'Do Not Enter' signs, and all Souliere told her was that it used to be a performance hall, but that it'd been off-limits for the past year.

Today, one of the back doors is ajar. Peering in, Rylie can see that it leads to a darkened backstage area filled with old props, abandoned costumes, and a few spools of manila rope used in the rigging system above the stage. A cleaner's cart is pushed to the side, the bright yellow mop bucket still steaming.

Guessing she has a few minutes to explore before the cleaner comes back and catches her trespassing, she slips inside. Amidst the junk—including an old stagecoach from a production of Cinderella, a balcony from which Juliet might call down to her Romeo, and an enormous wooden cross from Jesus Christ Superstar—there's a wall dedicated to cast and crew photographs from past productions.

Using the flashlight on her phone to get a better look, Rylie scans through the pictures, surprised to find Carriveau in several of them. Dressed in casual wear—jeans and a t-shirt in some shots, jeans and a simple cotton blouse in others—she seems much more relaxed than Rylie's so far known her to be around others. Although she usually dresses down on the weekends, Rylie's yet to see her in something as informal as a t-shirt; the weather's simply not warm enough.

Not only that, but she looks happy. Really happy. In a handful of pictures, she's even wearing her hair down, her dark mane cascading over her shoulders, completely unfettered

"Wow," Rylie mumbles to herself.

There are other recognizable faces in the pictures, too. She spots Adel Edwards, and Gabby, and a few others that she's come to know over the last few weeks, as well as a familiar-looking blonde: Kaitlyn Simmons. There's even a picture of Kaitlyn and

Carriveau together, their arms around each other's waists, Carriveau pressing a kiss against the side of Kaitlyn's head while Kaitlyn makes a kissy face for the camera.

Elsewhere, the wall is covered with graffiti. Students have signed their names in black marker pen, preserving their stamp on Larkhill for posterity, jotting down inspirational messages and well wishes to future students who might tread the boards here. Amongst the mess of scrawls, there's a black heart with the letters KS and VC inside it.

Kaitlyn Simmons and Vivienne Carriveau? Really? Rylie dismisses it and moves on. Thousands of students have come and gone from this school; those initials could belong to anybody. Indeed, there are many more hearts scattered about, memorializing a plethora of other romances, some angrily scrubbed out.

She dumps her backpack on the floor at the edge of the stage and approaches a piano-shaped mound covered by a tarp. Sure enough, when she flings back the moth-eaten canvas cloak, she unveils a grand piano in pristine condition.

Lifting the fallboard, she plinks a few keys, determines that it's still in tune, then sits down on the piano stool and begins to play, despite the risk of being caught. She starts off with a funeral dirge, but soon tires of it and moves into something much more upbeat: a song she wrote herself, in fact.

She's well into the middle of it before she senses movement in the periphery of her vision. She stops playing mid-keystroke and looks up, prepared to spout a hurried apology to the cleaner and make a swift exit, but it's not the cleaner standing at the edge of the stage next to her backpack, it's Carriveau.

"Continue," Carriveau prompts her. "*S'il te plaît.*"

She looks softer now than she did in the classroom, and Rylie obliges, playing the song out to its completion.

After the last note fades, "How did you know where to find me?"

"I didn't." Carriveau steps forward. "I heard music and came to admonish whichever unruly pupil had snuck in here to mess about."

"Am I in trouble?" Rylie keeps her eyes on the keys, tiptoeing her fingers over them.

"*Non, ma chérie.*" Carriveau walks around the piano. "Did you compose that yourself?"

Rylie nods, self-conscious.

"Why aren't you enrolled in music classes?"

"My parents think it's a waste of time." Rylie lowers the fallboard, covering the ivories.

"But you're so talented." Carriveau budges her over with a wiggle of her hips and sits on the stool beside her, facing away from the piano. "Haven't they heard you play?"

"They have, and they don't care." Still in a somber mood, Rylie drops her hands from the fallboard to her lap, her gaze lowering with them. "But thank you."

"I mean it." Carriveau reaches for one of her hands, weaving their fingers together. "I wish we had a piano in the house. You could serenade me."

Rylie tries to smile, but it doesn't stick. "So you're not angry with me anymore?"

"Angry with you?"

"You barely looked at me in class."

"How could I?" Carriveau winces, pained by the need to suppress her true feelings. "I can't even say your name without blushing."

"I disobeyed you this morning." Rylie remains downcast. "You think I'm impetuous, and impatient, and—"

"I think you're beautiful." Carriveau hooks Rylie's chin and turns her head. "You're intelligent, passionate, and exuberant—too exuberant. You disobeyed me, but believe me, the only anger I feel is toward myself."

"What for? *I* kissed *you*, not the other way around. You didn't do anything wrong."

Carriveau laughs. "Oh, my darling, I've done plenty wrong." She glances down at Rylie's lap, the hem of her skirt riding up several inches above her knees.

Running the tip of one manicured nail from Rylie's knee upward, she crumples the skirt, exposing the teen's smooth, flawless skin and the scratch marks still visible from last night's encounter in the laundry room.

"See?" She strokes her fingers over the faint pink lines, the skirt pulled so high it almost reveals Rylie's knickers. "I've been misbehaving dreadfully."

In response, Rylie parts her legs. It's only a few inches, but the invitation couldn't possibly be any more explicit—and Carriveau accepts it. She pushes Rylie's legs open wider and bends to kiss the grazed skin of her upper inner thigh. Her face buried there, she murmurs with pleasure when she inhales the sweet, musky scent of Rylie's sex.

"What are you doing to me, Rylie?" she mumbles, taking a pinch of Rylie's flesh between her teeth, nipping gently. "*Tu me rends folle!*" She tenders one more kiss, then raises her head. "You make me crazy!"

Rylie lifts up her skirt, baring the damp gusset of her knickers, coaxing Carriveau to return her lips to work, but Carriveau closes her eyes and shies away from temptation.

"You're making this very difficult for me. Do you realize that? I know well what you're feeling." She tugs on the hem of Rylie's skirt, covering her up. "But can't you see that you're moving this along much too fast? Promise me that you'll slow down. What happened this morning was just too much."

"It was only a kiss," Rylie protests. "I—"

"I don't give up my kisses so easily," Carriveau stops her. "And I don't appreciate having them taken from me. Now"—she checks the time on Rylie's watch—"your next class will be starting soon." She gets up off the stool. "*Allons-y.*" She urges Rylie up. "We should go. This place is out of bounds anyway."

"Why?" Rylie stands and straightens her skirt. "What's wrong with it?"

"There was an accident here last year," Carriveau answers vaguely, herding Rylie back toward the door they both crept in through.

"What kind of accident?"

"A girl lost her life." Carriveau ushers her out into the corridor, avoiding eye contact. "It was very tragic."

"Did you know her well?" Rylie pries, unaware that the nerve she's picking at is still incredibly raw.

Fortunately, thanks to a well-timed school bell, Carriveau is released from answering.

CHAPTER NINE

RYLIE, THE LAST STUDENT TO ARRIVE, RUSHES INTO her English Language class and slinks into the seat beside Gabby.

"This oughta be fun," Gabby grumbles, doodling daisies in her notebook. "I heard Miss Carriveau's been in a foul mood all day."

Rylie shrugs. "I was just with her. She seems fine now."

"Yeah? Is that 'cause she was giving you some more"—Gabby waggles her fiery eyebrows—"private lessons?" Grinning, she scooches back in her chair, parts her legs, and gyrates her hips, uttering a short burst of sex noises.

"Stop that!" Rylie slaps her arm. "Those private lessons were to help me catch up with this term's French syllabus," she lies. "I'm not having sex with Miss Carriveau!"

In the midst of that declaration, the noise level in the room drastically drops.

Cringing, Rylie swivels to face the door, knowing instinctively that Carriveau's standing there, having heard every outspoken word.

"No, you're not," the seemingly unflappable Housemistress confirms for the class as she closes the door behind her. "No matter how much you might want to."

The class erupts in laughter—entirely at Rylie's expense—but Carriveau takes it in her stride, letting them get a few good guffaws out before she restores order and forges on with the lesson.

Much to Rylie's relief, the incident soon seems forgotten. The sporadic muffled snickering dies down—stamped out by Carriveau's tight rein—and minds turn to coursework instead of gossip. That is, until Rylie puts her hand up to answer a question and is rewarded with a *"Très bien, ma chérie"* instead of a "Well done, Harcourt."

Carriveau corrects herself without pause, but the retraction doesn't stop a wave of jeering ooooohs from rippling around the room, completely drowning out whatever it is she says next. Of course, Adel doesn't join in; she's too busy fuming in the back row.

Then, the bell rings.

Forgetting their manners in the wake of such hilarity, the students rise from their chairs, gathering up books and bags, chattering amongst themselves without waiting to be dismissed.

"Ahem." Carriveau clears her throat, making them stop in their tracks. "Did I pause for breath and give you all the impression I was done speaking?"

Bums rapidly plunk back into seats.

"Merci." She begins again. "I have your marked assignments from last week, so collect them from me on your way out, and don't forget that your creative narratives are due in on Monday." She rises from her desk with a stack of papers in her arms, opens the classroom door, and prepares to release her ill-mannered pupils. "Now, you may leave as I call your names." She shuffles the assignments, holding out the one on top. "Adamson."

A girl in the back row gets up, collects her paper, and leaves, and Carriveau works her way down the stack, offering feedback where appropriate. It's no surprise to Rylie that she's the last student called, and she has no objection to waiting a few extra minutes for freedom if it means a few extra seconds alone with Carriveau.

"Pay special attention to my notes on the last page," Carriveau says, handing her a very respectable A-minus. "And I'll see you later, *ma chérie*." She winks, making light of her slip-up.

Out in the corridor, Rylie flicks through Carriveau's red pen notations, seeing that she's been caught on two misuses of a semi-colon, a typing error, and a few poor vocabulary choices. She flips to the back. Beneath a short commentary about her writing style, and possible improvements she could make, there's the most important thing of all: an invitation.

Dinner at the house tonight?

Around the corner from the classroom, Rylie stops in her tracks, unable to take her eyes off the page. In fact, she's so focused on Carriveau's words, and the promises they might hold, that Adel's able to completely blindside her.

She's shoved up against the wall before she can register the hostility in Adel's actions, and the air's knocked out of her lungs. She tries to draw breath, but can't. An intense, crushing pressure at her lower right side causes her to double over, wheezing.

Her first ever punch in the ribs.

Then, Adel's hand is on her throat, forcing her upright, pinning her to the wall.

"Stay away from Vivienne, *ma chérie*," she snarls, promptly storming off.

In over two weeks, those are the first words Adel's said to her.

Rylie lingers in the students' bathroom outside the refectory, staring at her reflection in the mirror. It's almost six o'clock, and Carriveau is probably already back at the house, making dinner for them both, expecting her arrival imminently.

She dithers, suddenly unsure of herself.

Every time she takes a breath, her chest hurts, and when she lifts her shirt to expose her ribs, she's not in the least bit surprised to find a large purple bruise forming in the spot where Adel thumped her. Is Carriveau worth that?

Duh.

Adel can suck it.

She snatches up her backpack and hightails it back to the house, hoping that her last minute arrival won't give away her momentary uncertainty. Stepping into the house without making any noise, she drops her backpack by the staircase and listens.

The house is quiet, except for the occasional clink of plates and cutlery, and there's an intoxicating smell drifting from the kitchen. Sneaking down the hallway, she peeks in on Carriveau, finding her standing by the stove, sautéing something in a shallow pan, her jacket slung over the back of a chair.

Looking pensive, a slight frown creasing her brow, the French woman checks her watch for the umpteenth time, the furrows of tension dissolving when she spies Rylie loitering in the doorway.

"*Bonsoir.*" She smiles. "I was afraid perhaps you weren't coming."

"You thought I'd stand you up?" Rylie cuts through the room and plants a firm kiss on Carriveau's cheek, broadening the older woman's smile, bringing on a flush of color.

"Well, you're just in time." The blushing Housemistress holds up two fingers. "This many minutes, then we eat."

"How did you know we'd have the house to ourselves tonight?" Rylie stays close, running a hand down Carriveau's back, tracing the curve of her spine.

"You know what day it is? Everybody loves the cook's cottage pie." Carriveau stirs and tosses the sizzling veggies. "Even Miss Ansell, and she's notoriously difficult to please."

"You didn't fancy it?" Rylie slips her hand lower, onto Carriveau's bum.

"Let's just say I can think of at least one thing in this house that I fancy a lot more." The Housemistress's blush intensifies, but she shows no desire to remove Rylie's hand from her posterior. "Anyway, I can only take so much of your English food."

At *least* one thing? Cynically, Rylie finds herself wondering how many other girls have ever been invited to dine with Carriveau alone.

Banishing that thought to the back of her mind, she nibbles on Carriveau's shoulder, continuing to fondle her bum. "What're you making?"

"*Ratatouille niçoise.* It's an Occitan dish from my home in *Provence, la Côte d'Azur.*"

"Sounds romantic."

"It's meant to be." Carriveau nuzzles her hair. "I want to apologize for being so hostile toward you in class. My personal feelings for you, no matter how complicated, should never be allowed to compromise my teaching."

"So you really do like me, then?"

"You can't tell?" Carriveau pushes her *derrière* into Rylie's hand.

"No, I mean ... more than the others?" Rylie gives her a squeeze. "More than Adel Edwards?"

"Why?" Carriveau takes the pan off the heat and dishes up their dinner, her expression giving nothing away. "Has she said something to you?"

Deciding it best not to mention their little spat in the corridor, Rylie shakes her head.

"She has an infatuation, that's all." Carriveau kisses Rylie's cheek, handing her a plate. "It's nothing for you to concern yourself with."

Rylie takes a seat next to Carriveau at one of the smaller tables, not sure if her ribs would agree that the matter is none of her concern. Still, she lets the subject go, satisfied enough to know that she's the one here with Carriveau while Adel eats with the masses in the refectory.

Indeed, now that she's here—feeling foolish for nearly chickening out—she's keen to make the most of this time alone, and so launches headlong into flattery and flirtation. "You have lovely hair. Why do you always wear it up so tight?"

"It makes me look stern." Carriveau bites into a chunk of green pepper. "It helps to compensate for the fact that I'm actually a bit of a soft touch."

"Fair enough." Rylie would give anything to have a better knowledge of her 'soft touch', but thinks better of verbalizing something so overt and cringe worthy. "I guess I really shouldn't complain anyway." She loads food onto her fork. "I've seen pictures of you with your hair down, and I reckon I'd have too much competition for your extracurricular affections if you walked around like that all the time."

"No, you wouldn't." Carriveau chuckles. "Lesbianism isn't contagious just because there aren't any boys around." She spears a piece of zucchini with her fork. "For most of the girls here, I'm merely an outlet for their adolescent hormones. I'm a convenient entity for them to thrust their attentions upon. By projecting their unfulfilled desires onto me, they feel less ... frustrated. I'm a pressure valve."

"So you don't mind everyone gawping at you all the time?"

Carriveau chases an evasive chunk of eggplant around her plate. "I sympathize. It's difficult to be cooped up in this place without the freedom to express yourself—particularly sexually—and I consider myself a surrogate for the girls here in many ways: a mother for most, a sexual object for some."

"Like Adel Edwards?"

"She wants to feel special—they all do. Desired even. My affection for them validates their sense of self-worth, but what they feel for me isn't real love.

They would balk at the thought of consummating their ridiculous flirtations with me in any physical way, and I've never, ever"—she emphasizes the word—"behaved with them as I have with you."

Rylie wonders where Adel's late night masturbation fits in with that, but says nothing.

"Is this why you asked about being my favorite?" Carriveau wonders. "You're worried that I might fancy all the girls in my house the way I fancy you?"

"I dunno. Maybe. Not really." Rylie pauses to rip a piece of tomato in half with her teeth, wishing it was Adel's jugular vein, annoyed that she'd let the bitch get to her.

"*Tu es la seule pour moi*," Carriveau assures her, dropping a soft kiss on her neck. "*Je promets.*"

You're the only one for me. I promise.

Still confused as to where Adel's busy fingers come into play, but disinclined to bring the matter up for fear of ruining what's promising to be a very intimate evening, Rylie concentrates on her food, clearing her plate in a few minutes flat. She wishes she could put Adel out of her mind altogether, but a dull ache in her ribs is a persistent reminder of their earlier altercation.

Misreading her silence as doubt, Carriveau makes another attempt to allay her concerns.

"I don't make a habit of this, if that's what you're thinking." She polishes off the last bite of her dinner. "What we're doing ... that is, what we both *want* to do is wrong. And not by Missus Bursnell's standards—let's be clear on that. I don't care one iota what our Headmistress considers unhealthy or improper. I speak only of British law, which I find myself evermore on the brink of violating."

Unsettled by her own declaration, Carriveau takes up both empty plates and loads them into the dishwasher. When she's done, she stays put, her back to the table, a rising uncertainty evident in her rigid posture.

"I'm sorry for this morning." Rylie slides out of her chair, intent on restoring Carriveau's mood. "I mean, I'm not sorry for kissing you," she continues, standing behind Carriveau, running both hands down her back. "But I am sorry for pushing myself on you." She sweeps her hands around Carriveau's waist, nestling her face close to her Housemistress's neck. "I just wanted to show you how serious I am about you, that's all." She nibbles on an unpierced earlobe. "I wasn't trying to be a dick."

Carriveau pivots in Rylie's arms, slightly separating herself. "Do you have any idea what tremendous trouble I could be in for this?"

"Yeah, I do." Rylie keeps a firm hold of her, squeezing and caressing her hips. "And if you thought my actions this morning made light of the risks you're taking with me, then I'm sorry for that as well." She acknowledges Carriveau's vulnerability, hoping to allay her concerns. "I shouldn't take a single second alone with you for granted."

Her conviction renewed by Rylie's sincerity, Carriveau takes her young student by the hand and leads her into the common room. *"Viens avec moi."*

Come with me.

After casting the room in the soft glow of a single lamp, she sinks into one of the large sofas and removes her shoes, tucking her feet up.

Not daring to presume anything, Rylie sits on the other end of the sofa, leaving a chaste distance between them, but when Carriveau unclips her hair and shakes her dark tresses loose, shifting sideways to face her, she shoves caution aside and makes a bid for closeness.

Shuffling nearer, she brushes her palm across Carriveau's cheek, fingering a lock of her silky mane, poring over her beauty, and Carriveau welcomes the advance. She wraps her arm around Rylie's shoulders, steeling herself to make an advancement of her own.

"Do you still want my lips?" she purrs, the question rhetorical.

She leans in for a kiss, teasing her would-be lover's lips apart with her own, pinching the teen's upper lip between her teeth, sucking it gently into her mouth. When that kiss breaks, she quickly reengages, flicking her tongue against Rylie's lips before closing her mouth over the whimpering seventeen-year-old's lower lip, tugging on it a little before releasing her and launching a third assault.

This time, she keeps her mouth open a moment longer, moaning her approval when Rylie's tongue darts out to meet hers before their crushing lips force a retreat. On the fourth lock, Carriveau slips her hand to the back of Rylie's neck, pulling her closer, their tongues meeting again, battling for entry into each other's mouths.

They kiss until breathless, parting reluctantly.

"A kiss is so much better when it's given freely, don't you think?" Carriveau guides Rylie's hand around her waist. "Much more erotic, *oui*?"

For several seconds, all Rylie can manage is a groan of contentment. She drops her head to Carriveau's neck and begins laying kisses there, starting below her ear and moving slowly lower, over her collar bone and lower still.

"How far can we go?" she mumbles between pecks, burying her face in Carriveau's cleavage, her hand traveling upward, from Carriveau's waist to her ribs, wavering at the underside of her breast. "If you tell me to stop, I will. I swear."

Carriveau is painfully aware that her nipples are tingling beneath her clothing, arousal seeping between her legs, her yearning undeniable. "*Mon amour*," she coos. "*Tu m'excites beaucoup.*" She stays Rylie's hand. "Do you know what that means?"

Rylie nods, lifting her head.

"You turn me on so much," Carriveau translates herself anyway, reaching gingerly for the top button of her blouse. "Is this really what you want?"

More nodding.

"Then give me your hand." Carriveau releases another button, steering Rylie inside her blouse, placing the teen's hand directly upon her breast.

Both women moan. Through the lace of the bra, Rylie can feel Carriveau's stiff nipple straining against the gossamer fabric, desperate for release.

"Shit, *Mademoiselle C—*"

"*Non, ne m'appelles plus Mademoiselle,*" Carriveau whispers against Rylie's ear, asking her to drop the formality. "When we're alone, call me *Vivienne, s'il te plaît.*"

She's about to coax Rylie's other hand inside her blouse when laughter and heavy footsteps outside signal that the first of the Upper and Lower Sixth girls of *la maison de Carriveau* are making their way down the garden path after dinner.

"Bollocks," Carriveau grumbles, wiping traces of her lipstick off Rylie's lips before retreating to the furthermost cushion and fixing her blouse. "Don't tell the others I made you dinner. The most they get from me is chicken soup when they're unwell."

At the last second, she slips her shoes on and heads for the kitchen to retrieve her jacket, appearing remarkably unruffled by the intrusion, even when she crosses paths with a steely-eyed Adel in the common room doorway.

"Wearing your hair different this evening, Miss?" the jealous teen asks out of turn.

Unperturbed by the question, as if such impudence is nothing out of the ordinary, Carriveau lies without missing a beat. "My clip broke."

From the sofa, shielded by it to some extent, Rylie watches the curt exchange with some interest and more than a little confusion, the role reversal painfully evident: Adel disapproving, Carriveau defiant.

Secreting the forgotten hairclip in her cardigan pocket to preserve the lie, Rylie pushes herself off the sofa and braves Adel's vicious glare as she shoves past her into the hallway, snatching up her backpack before ascending the stairs to the dorm.

That night, after lights out, she lies awake in bed, keeping herself vigilant, waiting for the commencement of Adel's carnal antics.

Waiting.

And waiting.

Growing bored, but waiting.

At the first telltale gasp, she flings back the covers and rises to her knees, peering over the wall of her cubicle toward the dormitory door, straining to see any movement beyond.

There is none.

She keeps her vigil until the last contented sigh, then dives back into her sheets, satisfied that whatever obscene hold Adel once had over Carriveau is now thoroughly broken.

CHAPTER TEN

WITHIN THE FIRST FIVE MINUTES OF BREAKFAST, one of the toasters catches fire, someone's porridge explodes in a microwave, and there's an uproar when it's discovered that there's no soy milk left in the refrigerator. In order words: typical morning chaos in Carriveau house.

Fifteen minutes later, however, one particular face still has yet to materialize.

"Where's Harcourt?" Carriveau snags Gabby's attention. "She's usually ready by now."

Gabby shrugs, chomping into a Pop-Tart. "Rylie said she wasn't feeling well." She talks with her mouth full of pastry, spitting crumbs. "I think she's gone back to bed."

"Want me to check on her?" Miss Ansell offers, privy to their conversation only on account of her proximity. "I can—"

"*Non.*" Carriveau is quick to quash the suggestion, but refrains from dashing upstairs. "This is my house, *n'est-ce pas?*" She heads calmly for the door, suppressing anything that could be interpreted as an undue amount of concern. "I'll go."

With forced nonchalance, she climbs the staircase and enters the Lower Sixth dormitory, finding Rylie groomed, but not dressed, lying face down on her bed, naked beneath her cotton pajamas, the cheeks of her bum outlined clearly behind the thin, pale fabric.

"*Qu'est-ce que tu as?*" Carriveau unbuttons her jacket, shrugs it off her shoulders, and drapes it over the cubicle wall. "What's the matter with you? Are you feeling unwell?"

Rylie groans, but doesn't move. "I'm sorry. I'll be up in a minute."

Hesitating at the thin yellow line, Carriveau takes one look out into the hall, makes certain that she can't hear any footsteps, then breaches the cubicle boundary.

"Will you tell me what's wrong?" She perches on the edge of Rylie's bed.

Covering for the fact that her ribcage has her in such a state of agony that she can't draw breath without causing herself excruciating pain, Rylie concocts a fib.

She rolls onto her back, wincing. "Girl stuff, that's all."

"Cramps? *Es-tu sûre?*" Carriveau leans over her. "May I fetch you something? Anything?"

Rylie shakes her head. "I took painkillers. Just waiting for them to kick in."

"Is there nothing I can do for you?" Carriveau presses the back of her hand to Rylie's forehead, then her cheeks, checking her temperature. "A hot water bottle, perhaps?" She transfers her hand to Rylie's abdomen, applying only a slight pressure.

Rylie squeals, tensing and jerking, flinching from Carriveau's touch. She tries to turn away, but Carriveau grips her shoulder and holds her to the bed, yanking up her pajama top, revealing the angry purple bruise on her lower ribs.

"*Mon Dieu!*" the Housemistress cries in horror. "What happened?!"

"It's nothing." Rylie grimaces, trying to get comfortable.

"Were you fighting?" Carriveau grazes Rylie's injured torso with her fingertips. "Please tell me you haven't been getting yourself involved in any nonsense?"

Rylie shakes her head. "There's been no nonsense, I promise."

"Is this the reason you're lying here in bed?" Carriveau caresses the teen's bare skin. "I have to make a note of this in the house accident and injury book." Her mind whirs through protocol. "And I should inform your parents."

"I wouldn't," Rylie cautions her. "They'd go ape-shit, and I don't want them to cause any unnecessary trouble."

"Have you seen the nurse at least?" Carriveau keeps mothering. "Visits with her are confidential. I can write you a note for your first class so that you can go straight to the medical center."

"I don't want to make a fuss."

"You're not making a fuss. *I'm* making a fuss, and you're going to do as you're told. Is that understood, *ma chérie*?"

Rylie smirks, amused to hear the stern edge of Carriveau's voice juxtaposed with such a tender endearment, the odd combination sparking a shallow fit of giggles that's abruptly abated by the discomfort in her chest.

"Oh, my love." Carriveau bends to kiss the heart of the bruise. "You must see the nurse."

As her lips make contact, she feels Rylie's fingers slip around the back of her neck, enticing her to continue. Murmuring her willingness, she plants kisses around Rylie's bellybutton, flicking her tongue in it before moving her mouth higher, finally pausing at the hem of Rylie's bunched-up pajama top, toying with the buttons.

"You can if you want." Rylie reads her thoughts. "I'm naked underneath."

Carriveau falters.

"Here"—Rylie undoes the buttons herself—"let me show you." She peels back the lightweight cotton, displaying her naked breasts.

"*Oh, Seigneur!*" Carriveau exclaims in a hushed voice, admiring Rylie's adolescent body.

Her nipples are rigid and swollen, begging to be kissed, the surrounding areolae puffed up. Both breasts are full and round; they're two small handfuls.

Trembling uncontrollably, Carriveau trails a finger down Rylie's chest, between both delightful mounds, over soft, milky skin.

"I wish they were bigger." Rylie looks down at herself. "More like yours."

"Oh, no," Carriveau coos, transfixed. "They fit you perfectly."

She scoops one into her hand, gasping at the sensation of Rylie's firm, warm flesh, and quickly brings her mouth to the other. She sucks the nipple into her mouth, pulling on it, nipping it, swirling her tongue around it.

"I need you," she mumbles, kissing her way back down Rylie's body. "I want more of you." She reaches the waistband of Rylie's pajama bottoms. "I can't resist you." She gives one sharp downward tug on the waistband, baring the top of Rylie's shaved mons.

She drops a kiss there, gripping the pajama bottoms with both hands as Rylie raises her hips and whimpers, urging her to do away with the clothing and fuck her. But then …

Voices herald the unwelcome return of three Lower Sixth girls, and Carriveau recoils like a frightened animal. She stands up, abruptly and unexpectedly revealing her presence to the perplexed students. Not only is it a shock for them to see her there, but to see her inside someone's cubicle, presumably on the bed, is a jaw-dropping sight indeed.

Flustered, Carriveau strives to regain her poise. "If you're not sick, you have to get up," she barks at Rylie, straightening her blouse. "No more moping, Harcourt."

Her cheeks burning, she snatches up her jacket and hurries toward the door, the three girls staring at her, struck silent by the heavy tension in the room.

"*Qu'est-ce que vous regardez?*" she snaps at them. "*Que voulez-vous?*"

What are you staring at? What do you want?

All three shake their heads and avert their eyes.

"Hurry up and get ready, else you'll be late," Carriveau warns, striding out of the room.

She locks herself away in her study, but gets little more than ten precious minutes alone before she's required to perform her morning uniform inspections.

As is now routine, Rylie takes her place at the back of the line, catching Carriveau's eye at intervals, flashing her sly smiles. When her turn comes, Carriveau makes sure she looks presentable, but tenders no forehead kiss. Instead, she takes a quick look around for Miss Ansell, then checks her watch.

"Would you like to come into my study for a few minutes?"

"Why?" Rylie feigns confusion. "Have I been a naughty girl?"

Holding back laughter, Carriveau takes Rylie by the hand and leads her away. "Let's not start that."

She flings open the door to her study and stops dead in her tracks. Miss Ansell is sitting in front of her desk, looking right at them—and at their entwined fingers.

Carriveau drops Rylie's hand. "May I help you, Miss Ansell?"

"It's the fifteenth of the month." Miss Ansell waggles a notebook at her. "We need to go over the house ordering, and I need your permission to call a plumber. There's a broken tap in the Upper Sixth bathroom."

Trying her best to appear unfazed, Carriveau takes a deep breath. "One moment," she commands Rylie to wait, then crosses to her desk, fills out a Hall Pass, and hands it off to her. "See the nurse before your first class, yes? No dillydallying."

Intent on behaving as if nothing's amiss, Carriveau gives Rylie a peck on the forehead before sending her on her way.

"You're going too far with her," Miss Ansell criticizes once they're alone.

"I kiss all my girls in that manner." Carriveau shrugs it off.

"And the rest?"

Carriveau sits at her desk, her jaw tight, taking a moment to answer. "It means nothing."

Miss Ansell regards Carriveau closely: her tear-filled eyes, her clenched teeth, her taut lips, two fingers pressed against them, as if physically holding her emotions inside.

"Are you ... ? Not again?" Miss Ansell shakes her head despairingly. "You need to get out of here and find yourself a woman."

"I can't; it would complicate my relationship with the children. There would never be the time to devote myself to this house, both of my classes, and to a girlfriend. One of those would surely suffer, and I wouldn't be doing my job properly if I didn't put the children first."

"Just as long as you remember that's what they are: children."

"The girls in this house are young women," Carriveau becomes defensive. "And Rylie's seventeen."

"But you're her teacher! *You* can't have her."

That seems to hit home.

"It's a lapse, that's all." Carriveau shuffles papers, distracting her mind. "I'll fix it."

"See that you do." Miss Ansell lets a heavy silence drop. "I'm sure you don't want to see this end like the other."

Carriveau sits alone in her office, no sound but that of a softly ticking clock and the creak of her chair as she shifts and opens up her laptop. Accessing Larkhill's student records, she types the name 'Harcourt' into a search field and brings up Rylie's class schedule.

Right now, Rylie's in a psychology lesson.

In half an hour, she has a free period.

Clicking a link for student contact information, Carriveau scrolls through Rylie's home address, her parents home and cell phone numbers, other emergency contacts, and then gets to Rylie's e-mail address and personal cell phone. Retrieving her own cell phone from a pocket in her jacket, she taps out a message.

> **Come to me after class. I'm in my office. V.C.**

She sets the phone down, not expecting to receive a response. A second later, it buzzes.

> **OK**

Scowling, she responds:

> **Don't text during class.**

The prompt reply:

> **Don't distract me during class ;-)**

Smiling for the first time since her conversation with Miss Ansell, Carriveau sets the phone aside again. Unfortunately, her cheer is short-lived. She can't help but think about all the things she should say to Rylie when the excitable teen arrives. Starting with: "I'm afraid we can't keep doing this. I've let it escalate much too far, and I shouldn't have. I'm sorry for that. I let myself get carried away with you, and it has to stop."

Then: "None of this can happen again. You must find a way to be happy with things as they are, or I'll have to insist that you be transferred to another house."

Even as she thinks it, she knows those words will never cross her lips. She pushes them out of her mind, losing track of the time as she battles with her conscience, and long before she's ready for it, there comes a knock at the door.

"*Entrez!*" She looks up as Rylie enters, her heavy thoughts lifting upon first sight of the girl. "Darling, how did it go with the nurse this morning? What did she say?" She invites Rylie to sit in front of her desk.

"She reckons I have a cracked rib, but says it's nothing to worry about unless I start having any difficulty breathing." Rylie dumps her backpack on the floor and plonks into one of the two available chairs, rattling a pill bottle she pulls from her cardigan pocket. "She gave me some painkillers and told me to take it easy for six weeks."

"Is there anything I can do for you?" Carriveau gets up from behind her desk and moves to the chair beside her favorite pupil.

"Well, now that you mention it"—Rylie turns her chair to face her Housemistress—"there is this massage technique she told me about, to help take my mind off the pain. She said I could do it myself, but it's better if I can find someone else to do it for me."

"Of course." Carriveau strokes Rylie's arm. "What is it?"

"It's simple." Rylie prepares to demonstrate. "First, you put your fingers together like this"—she pairs her fore and middle fingers, curling them upward—"then you insert them in my—"

Carriveau gives the teen's arm a light slap. "Very funny." She rolls her eyes.

Rylie giggles, clutching her ribs. "Worth a try, I reckon."

"You're incorrigible," Carriveau scolds her. "And I wish you'd tell me who did this to you." She lays a hand over Rylie's bruise. "Larkhill does not tolerate bullies."

"I'm not being bullied," Rylie assures her. "Some people are just sore losers."

"This was a game?"

"Not to me." Rylie smiles warmly, keeping the truth of the event to herself, afraid that if Carriveau were to find out the injury was caused in a clash between her two suitors then she might put an end to their dalliance.

Though still concerned, Carriveau accepts that some matters simply would not benefit from the intervention of a teacher—indeed, that they could even be exacerbated by it—so she lets the subject go, turning her mind instead to a rather more upbeat topic.

"I have something for you." She dials up a smile and bends over her desk, rummaging through loose papers. "It's here somewhere."

Rylie angles her chair for a better view of Carriveau's posterior. "Keep looking. Take your time."

"You like my *derrière*?" Carriveau gives her rump a little shake before resuming her search. "Ah!" She plucks a leaf of paper from under her laptop. "Sign-ups ended a month ago, but I've made special arrangements for you."

"That sounds like an exception." Rylie takes the proffered page, barely restraining her excitement when she realizes it's a flyer for the after-class music club.

"I know I said I wasn't going to make any of those." Carriveau returns to her side. "But one more could hardly hurt, and I want an excuse to hear you play again."

"I have something for you, too." Rylie fishes around in her backpack, pulling out a writing assignment bound in a plastic folder. "Will you read this over for me? It's my English homework. My creative narrative."

Carriveau takes it from her, laughing.

"What's so funny?" Rylie frowns.

"Nothing, darling. It's just I'd rather I wasn't your—" She stops herself, sadness invading. "That is, I'd prefer it if my obligations to you were different. *Tu comprends?*"

"Acutely." Rylie places a hand on Carriveau's stockinged knee. "Do you want me to drop French again? Would it be easier for you if you taught me less?"

"Oh, *mon amour*. Trust me, if these feelings of ours endure, and the time comes for one of us to make a sacrifice, that one shall not be you. The burden of responsibility in this is mine, and mine alone."

"That hardly seems fair." Rylie works her fingers beneath the hem of Carriveau's skirt.

"It's as it should be. But in the meantime, we'll continue as normal and let things play out." Carriveau steals a peck on the lips. "After all, we haven't yet done anything too terrible." Another peck. "So I'll read your homework this evening." One more lingering peck. "I'll give you my notes in the morning." Her eyes twinkle. "In my study."

Rylie's mind flashes back to this morning's scuppered attempt to harness a few moments of privacy, and to the angered look on Miss Ansell's face.

"What if someone twigs?" She tastes Carriveau's lipstick on her lips. "Other teachers, I mean."

"Who? Miss Ansell?" Carriveau shakes her head. "Don't worry about her. We'll have to be more careful around the house, but generally speaking, I learnt a while ago that the more you struggle to conceal something, the more obvious it becomes. So just relax and think nothing of it, then nor will anyone else."

"Spoken like a repeat offender," Rylie jokes.

The comment is intended to be lighthearted, but Carriveau doesn't take it that way.

"I know it goes against all good sense and reason for me to let this happen." Her mood dulls. "But I don't want to stop being close to you, Rylie. I love—"

There's a sharp knock at the door, and Adel barges in without waiting to be invited.

"*Alors là! Où sont tes manières?* Where are your manners, Edwards?" Carriveau recovers quickly, retracting her own hand and pushing Rylie's off her knee, hastily retreating behind her desk. "Thank you for this, Harcourt." She sets Rylie's homework in front of her. "We'll speak later."

Rylie accepts the brisk dismissal without complaint, but Carriveau's interrupted words ring in her ears for the remainder of the afternoon, a hundred different questions forming around them.

I love—

I love ... what? You? This? Something else?

Trust Adel Edwards to ruin it.

CHAPTER ELEVEN

LONG AFTER LIGHTS OUT, CARRIVEAU UNCORKS A bottle of wine she's been keeping hidden in her private quarters and sits down in the common room, sipping from a mug. She props her feet up on the coffee table, rests Rylie's homework against her thighs, and dons her reading glasses.

The first line causes her to choke on her booze.

My orgasm hits me hard, her fingers deep inside me, probing every inch of my hungry, gushing sex, coaxing a cry of pleasure from my lips ...

It goes on, transitioning into a flashback that sets up the introduction of the two main characters: a young, blue-eyed blonde and a somewhat older, green-eyed brunette.

Subtle, she giggles to herself. Really subtle.

Aroused and intrigued, she keeps reading, concluding that Rylie must be sexually experienced. Her writing is too explicit, and much too accurate to be the work of an overactive imagination ... surely ... hopefully.

Carriveau sets her mug of wine on the arm of the sofa and leans back, sliding her hips forward, causing her skirt to bunch around her thighs.

She reads on.

Her cheeks are burning, the flush spreading to her chest, her cunt throbbing impatiently. Clutching the hem of her skirt, she relaxes her knees, continuing to read as she slips a hand between her legs, tickling her fingers over her core.

She's sopping wet.

Groaning with need, she tucks Rylie's porn under her arm, grabs the bottle and her shoes with one hand, her mug with the other, and tiptoes upstairs. As she grapples with the lock on the door to her private quarters, she hears the floor creaking behind her.

"Vivienne …"

Carriveau turns to face Rylie, stifling a gasp at the teen's slender form. She's clad only in a white cotton nightdress and knickers, erect nipples and dark pink areolae showing through, tenting out the fabric at her bust.

"What are you doing up so late?" she asks, realizing that she's staring, jerking her eyes up. "Do you need something?"

Rylie doesn't answer, her own eyes drawn to the wine, knowing there's not supposed to be any alcohol in the house.

"Sshhh." Carriveau puts her fingers to her lips. "Our secret."

She swings open the door to her rooms and doesn't bother to close it behind her when she enters, leaving it flung wide: a silent invitation.

What happens next is now entirely up to Rylie, the doorway simply a portal offering countless unspoken possibilities—and the besotted student isn't about to pass any of them up.

She steps inside, lingering at the threshold of Carriveau's modest living area, a bedroom to the right, and a bathroom to the left. The bedroom door is ajar, and through it, Rylie can see a queen-sized bed draped in silk sheets.

"Don't hover." Carriveau tosses her shoes on the floor and lets down her hair. "Either you're in, or you're out. Make up your mind."

She flops onto a sofa at the edge of the room and pours herself another mug of wine, setting the bottle and the porn on a tempered glass coffee table.

Facing Rylie, she drapes one arm over the back of the sofa, the other nursing the mug in her lap, her pelvis angled forward, her legs crossed, leaning into the cushions, waiting for the teen to make a decision.

Rylie pushes the door closed.

Smiling, Carriveau brings the mug to her lips, taking a sip. "You wrote me porn."

"Did you like it?" Rylie moves toward her.

"You know I can't submit it to the school, don't you?" Carriveau's wicked smile sticks. "You'll have to write me something else for class."

"It wasn't meant for the school," Rylie confesses, sinking into the cushions beside her. "It was only meant for you."

Carriveau swirls the wine in her mug, trying to downplay her arousal. "I have to ask ... do you write from experience?"

"You want to know if I'm a virgin?"

Carriveau's stomach somersaults at the thought. "I'm curious about your expertise." She fingers the rim of her mug. "You write with a certain ... precision."

"I haven't been a virgin in almost two years." Rylie edges nearer. "Is my lack of innocence a disappointment to you? Or does it excite you?"

Carriveau raises her gaze, her pupils dilated on account of her mild inebriation, intoxicated as much with the moment as she is with the wine. "Quite honestly, it relieves me."

Rylie shuffles closer still, moving slowly in case the overture is met with rejection.

It isn't.

She maneuvers alongside Carriveau, her bare thighs grazing silk stockings. Reaching forward, she plucks Carriveau's mug from her hand. The consenting Housemistress makes no attempt to hold onto it, and says nothing when she takes a sip from it and sets it down on the coffee table.

Growing bolder by the second, Rylie grabs Carriveau by the ankle and swings one of her legs onto the sofa, spreading her thighs.

"Rylie!" Carriveau squeals, taken aback by the girl's audacity.

Another squeal is quick to follow as Rylie seizes her hips and yanks her forward, kneeling between her parted legs, bending over her.

Instinctively, Carriveau relaxes into the sofa, lying further and further back with every inch of Rylie's advancement until the pair are horizontal. Rylie, above and in control, lowers herself into a kiss and Carriveau closes her eyes in anticipation of it, allowing herself to be seduced. Then, Rylie thrusts forward, slamming her pelvis against Carriveau's sex.

And again.

And again.

Her ribs are screaming, but she keeps going.

Carriveau grunts every time Rylie crushes into her, and she demonstrates her appreciation by grinding her hips up to meet every lunge, reaching down to grasp Rylie's bum, pulling her tighter, nearing orgasm from the mere simulation of penetrative sex.

Craving the release, she digs her nails into Rylie's flesh, her body tensed for climax, then ... Rylie slows down. Carriveau is about to growl out a complaint when she feels Rylie's hands on her chest, unbuttoning her blouse, intent on freeing her breasts.

To that end, Rylie gives the satin a firm tug, exposing the bra beneath. Brimming with lust, she's in such a hurry to disrobe her Housemistress that she fumbles the front clasp on the bra three times before she's finally able to release it.

"Oh, thank god," she whimpers, casting her eyes on Carriveau's naked breasts. "They're real." She takes one in her hand, massaging it firmly. "They are real, aren't they? You're so soft."

Carriveau laughs. "Yes, they're all mine. You thought I had fake tits?"

"You're stacked. I was *afraid* you had fake tits."

Carriveau starts to laugh again, but the sound gets caught in her throat, turning to a stunted squeak

128

as Rylie brings her hot mouth to the other breast and starts suckling on her.

"You're breathtaking," Rylie murmurs, moving from one breast to the other, both delicious pink nipples pointed to the ceiling. "So gorgeous."

They begin kissing in earnest, a flurry of hungry tongues and lips. Carriveau's hand finds its way under Rylie's nightdress, caressing her silky thigh, while Rylie's hand starts traveling downward, from breasts, to waist, to ...

Carriveau breaks off the kiss.

Rylie's heart sinks. She went too far again?

"I can't give you everything you want from me," Carriveau maintains feebly, panting heavily. "Not tonight; not like this. I wish I could."

Ignoring that, Rylie tenders another kiss and lifts Carriveau's hand to her breast, encouraging Carriveau to fondle her over her nightdress.

Reacting without conscious thought, Carriveau arches her back into Rylie, accepting the sweep of a furtive hand over her waist and hip, pushing her legs further apart.

"Rylie ..." She moans again, Rylie's lips breaking away from hers to travel south.

While lips and tongue trail over her neck and chest, she feels a sure hand creep up her inner thigh, seeking out her throbbing, impatient sex.

"That's enough," Carriveau pleads.

Rylie doesn't stop.

"*Ça suffit*," Carriveau whispers more forcefully.

Rylie continues regardless.

"*Arrête!*" Carriveau pushes Rylie away, losing her composure for a brief moment. "Stop, stop, stop!" She tears her hand away from Rylie's breast and holds the teen's wandering, tickling fingers at bay before they can discover her damp knickers. "This is too much." She forces Rylie's hand out from between her legs. "This is too much, too soon."

129

"Why do you keep saying that?" Rylie rocks back on her heels. "You want me to touch you, so why won't you let me?"

Carriveau wriggles into the corner of the sofa, sitting upright. "I don't want to have sex with you, Rylie!"

She regrets the words as soon as they've left her lips, even before the hurt shows itself on Rylie's face. Calming herself, she shifts to sit properly on the sofa, closing her legs and pulling the hem of her skirt down to cover the tops of her stockings.

"*Excuse-moi*," she recants. "What I mean to say is: that's not *all* I want."

"That's not all *I* want, either." Rylie slumps next to her.

"Are you sure?" Carriveau hooks up her bra, trapping her breasts back inside. "*Passe-moi l'expression*: I'm not a fascination fuck." She snatches up her mug, downs every drop in it, then pours a refill.

"That's what you think this is? You think I only want you because you're my teacher?" Rylie throws her head back against the sofa. "For god's sake, I love you!"

Carriveau winces, wishing she could believe that. "Oh, darling. You barely know me."

"How can you say that? After all the hours we've spent together, talking about anything and everything that had nothing to do with school."

Still, Carriveau won't budge. "We need to wait," she mumbles, already halfway through her refilled mug.

"Oh, yeah?" Rylie's patience crumbles, feeling irked enough to put Carriveau on the spot, testing out a suspicion that's been rolling around in her head for weeks. "How long did you make Kaitlyn Simmons wait?"

In a split second, Rylie realizes her mistake. The utterance of the girl's name has a much stronger effect than she'd intended, Carriveau's entire mood changing instantly.

"Where did you hear that name?" Her voice is cold and monotone, her lips pinched tightly together, the light in her eyes extinguished.

Rylie shrugs. "Everywhere. Who is she?"

"A former student of this house." Carriveau downs more wine. "But she's gone now, and I don't see any point in—"

"Was there something between you?" Rylie cuts in, desperate to learn the truth.

"I think you already know." Carriveau seeks solace in her mug. "Don't make me say it."

Rylie won't press for details, but she needs to ask, "Did she love you?"

Carriveau takes a long sip of wine before answering. "More than I knew."

Her expression softens, sorrow surfacing in place of the anger, and Rylie feels guilty for having been the cause. In an attempt to salvage something between them, she slips a hand onto Carriveau's thigh, hoping to tempt her back into intimacy.

"I'm sorry. I—"

"You have to go." Carriveau removes Rylie's hand from her lap. "Get back to your dormitory and go to sleep. *Bonne nuit.*"

Pained by Carriveau's pain, and not knowing how she can help, Rylie does as she's told. She leaves her faintly sobbing Housemistress alone with her wine and slips out into the hallway, expecting to tiptoe back into bed without alerting anyone to her absence.

But no such luck.

Adel's standing in the hall, arms folded, her hateful eyes following Rylie every step of the way from Carriveau's door into the dormitory.

Rylie groans and shifts, rising into consciousness at the sensation of pressure on the edge of her bed, the weight causing a dip in the mattress. She rolls onto her back to confront the shadowy mass, half thinking it might be an irate Adel, come to bust another rib, or smother her with a pillow. But one whiff of the sweet perfume hanging on the air, along with the faint aroma of shampoo and the pungent scent of red wine, and she knows precisely who her midnight visitor is.

It's Carriveau.

The French woman is silhouetted by a single beam of moonlight spilling in through a skylight window, and as Rylie's eyes adjust, she can see that her blouse is still partially unbuttoned, her bra-clad breasts entirely visible beneath.

"Wh—"

"Sshhh," Carriveau whispers, leaning over the bed, pressing two fingers to Rylie's lips. "Don't make a sound."

Those two fingers quickly find their way beneath the covers, diving up Rylie's nightdress and inside her underwear with no hint of hesitation or insecurity.

Rylie holds her breath, keeping back a yowl as Carriveau's cold fingertips come into contact with her hot flesh. Unable to vocalize her approval, she opens her legs wider and brings a hand to Carriveau's, encouraging her Housemistress down through a strip of wiry hair on her mons, beyond a piercing in her clitoral hood, and onward to her opening.

When Carriveau's fingers slip deeper into her valley, Rylie floods in seconds.

"*Mon Dieu!*" Carriveau murmurs, nibbling on a delicate earlobe, holding back another exclamation of pleasure as she pushes her fingers all the way inside, exploring Rylie's deep sex. "You're so wet."

And tight.

And hot.

And perfect.

She spills a string of hushed compliments, all *en français*, and only some of which Rylie understands. Then, at the first tiny noise that escapes Rylie's lips, Carriveau smothers her mouth with a wine-flavored kiss, the remainder of the bottle consumed just minutes ago.

She's drunk.

Her judgment's skewed.

"Where is it?" she whispers against Rylie's ear.

"Where's what?" Rylie mutters huskily, approaching climax already.

"Your toy."

Rylie unlocks her private drawer in the bedside table and fishes out a seven-inch dildo as Carriveau flings back the covers and clambers onto the bed. The tipsy Housemistress then proceeds to withdraw her fingers from Rylie's cunt and wet the thick cock with her mouth before pushing the tip between Rylie's labia, finding her opening and sliding through it.

Rylie clutches fistfuls of the bed sheets, toes curling as Carriveau fucks her gently, lifting her hips to penetrate her deeper, moving harder and faster.

In under five minutes, the teen starts to shake, barely breathing, bucking and writhing beneath her Housemistress.

"I'm coming!" she whispers frantically.

Carriveau's fucking continues unabated, bringing Rylie's orgasm to full force. In the final moments, Rylie pulls Carriveau against her, tucking her head against Carriveau's shoulder, biting down on the first area of exposed skin she finds, muffling the arrival of her peak.

When it's over, they release each other, Rylie's cunt contracting and pulsing, Carriveau's neck stinging with a strangely pleasurable pain.

"I *do* love you," Rylie insists.

Carriveau plants a kiss on her. "I want that to be true." More kisses. "I want that more than anything."

She pulls the dildo out and sets it on the bedside table, then pads barefoot out of the dormitory, walking on her tippy-toes, her stealthy exit and her illicit encounter with Rylie not going unnoticed by all.

Lying awake in her bed, Adel glowers at Carriveau's ghostly, retreating form.

CHAPTER TWELVE

WEEKENDS ARE ODD DAYS. SEEING CARRIVEAU wearing tight jeans and a fitted cotton shirt is always a pleasure, but Saturdays are filled with sports competitions, homework, and other time-sucking activities that leave little time for flirtation.

After the luxury of being woken an hour later than usual, the Upper and Lower Sixth girls of Carriveau house are ushered up and onto the playing field to support their house's lacrosse team in a friendly competition against a rival sixth form house.

While Rylie takes a seat with Gabby on one of the many wooden benches surrounding the field, her damaged ribcage forcing her to watch instead of participate, banned from inclusion in all sports until her body is healed, she finds her attention divided between the pre-game warm-ups and Carriveau.

Standing with a small cluster of other Housemistresses and their Deputies, she's sipping from a travel mug of hot coffee, her neck wrapped in a thin woolen scarf bearing the colors of her house—as are the others, with the colors of their respective houses.

Rylie's cunt spasms every time she looks at her, the memory of last night causing ripples of arousal to flutter through the very deepest part of her core, those muted sensations rising to a pulsing lust as Carriveau separates from the clique and rejoins her house.

"*Puis-je m'asseoir ici?*" she asks her girls to make room on the bench, wriggling her bum in between Rylie and Gabby, squashing herself tightly between them. "Mmm, snug." She shakes her hips from side to side, bumping and rubbing against the two accommodating teens.

She settles herself just in time, the whistle blowing and the game commencing. Three goals and one foul later, and she feels Rylie's leg twitching against her thigh, the benched player tapping her foot agitatedly on the grass.

"How soon can you play again?" Carriveau nudges her, detecting envy and frustration in her tensed muscles.

"Two months." Rylie bites on a fingernail. "Their right wing defense sucks."

"What's your position?"

"Second home," Rylie answers seriously, then giggles. "We're still talking about lacrosse, yeah?"

Carriveau keeps her eyes on the game, answering quietly. "Second home is an important offensive position on the field, *non*? Your ball handling skills must be excellent."

Rylie pulls a face. "Yuck!"

Carriveau smirks into her travel mug. "You're naked, by the way." She takes a sip, then peers down at her best girl. "Why aren't you wearing house colors yet?"

Rylie glances at Carriveau's scarf, then back to the field. "I'm waiting for my parents to send me my allowance so I can buy one. Don't worry, I'm not planning on defecting."

"Here"—Carriveau laughs, unwrapping her scarf from her neck—"you can wear mine."

As she pulls the scarf off, she bares a purple, bite-shaped bruise at the edge of her neck, right above her collar bone.

"Wow, Miss." Gabby eyeballs it. "What happened to you?"

Despite distinctly visible teeth impressions, Carriveau adjusts the collar of her blouse to cover it and lays the blame on her clumsiness.

"Okay, you caught me." She balances her mug between her knees and wraps her arms around Rylie and Gabby, drawing them close, pretending that she's letting them in on a secret. "I might've had a special bottle of wine stashed away in the house, I might've overindulged somewhat, and then had myself *un petite accident* last night." Her gaze lands on Rylie.

"A little accident?" Rylie glares incredulously at her. "Is that what it was?"

"Some accident," Gabby snorts, turning her attention back to the game.

Carriveau has no opportunity to respond.

"Yeah"—Rylie jerks herself free of her Housemistress—"some fucking accident." She balls up the scarf, chucks it into Carriveau's lap, and storms off.

Angered and annoyed, she leaves the playing field behind and seeks refuge in the main sports building, keen to be alone. She wanders aimlessly down the halls, checks her phone, texts a few people, reminds her parents to send her the allowance they promised, and finally winds up in a room full of sports memorabilia.

Some of Larkhill's former pupils have gone on to win Olympic medals, their achievements documented here, alongside their school medals. In one trophy cabinet, there are several pictures of a blonde girl, some newspaper clippings, and a first place trophy that was awarded for winning a national gymnastics competition, donated to the school by the parents of the winning child: Kaitlyn Simmons.

"Comparing?"

Adel's voice startles her.

"What?" Rylie scrunches up her face. "Sod off."

"Seeing how you measure up against the old *petite amie*? You both have blonde hair and blue eyes; I guess Vivienne likes that." Adel sidles up to her. "You're shorter than Kaitlyn, but you have bigger tits." She reaches around and grabs Rylie's left breast.

"Fuck you!" Rylie smacks Adel's hand away, shifting out of her grasp. "What's your problem?!" She spins to face her unwelcome groper.

"Lately, my problem is you." Adel gives her a push, jabbing her sore ribs.

"Why?" Rylie stands her ground, masking her pain. "What did I ever do to you? Besides exist."

"I told you to stay away from her." Adel keeps advancing. "It's for your own good."

"Oh, yeah? How's that?" Emboldened by the presence of several ceiling-mounted security cameras intended to guard the priceless memorabilia, Rylie squares up to her aggressor. "Are you gonna hit me again?" She straightens her shoulders, standing tall. "Go on. Give it a try. Let's see where it gets you this time." She invites Adel to thump her, making sure she's positioned for the cameras. "Suspension, you reckon? Expulsion maybe? Whatever happens, you sure as fuck won't scare me away from Vivienne."

"Hey, I'm only trying to do you a favor." Adel backs up, holding both hands in the air, signaling no threat. "I don't want to see you end up like poor old Kaitlyn, that's all." She juts out her lower lip, faking sorrow. "That would be such a tragic loss."

"I don't get it." Rylie frowns. "What happened to Kaitlyn? I thought she left."

"She did." Adel folds her arms, adopting a smug grin. "In a coroner's van."

Rylie's stomach twists and turns, churning upside down and threatening to toss up her breakfast. Carriveau isn't just heartbroken, she's mourning. No wonder she's so afraid to let go.

"Was Kaitlyn the girl who had the accident in the old performance hall?" Rylie asks then, the pieces now fitting together.

"Accident?" Adel snorts. "That was no accident. The stupid bitch killed herself."

After four hours of solid schoolwork, the words on the pages start blurring together. The study room—thirty individual cubicles surrounding one large table—is quiet, all other students having retired from their homework already this evening. Most are now to be found watching television in the common room, or mucking about in the dormitories. But not Rylie.

Seated at the main table, she's now halfway through her second attempt at a creative narrative for Carriveau's English Language class, and her concentration is waning. She yawns, but soldiers on, determined to hide herself away until it's time to head up to the dorm for bed.

She doesn't hear the door open and close. The first hint she has of Carriveau's presence is the scent of her perfume, followed by the faint sound of breathing.

"*Mon amour* ..." the beautiful French woman calls demurely to her from the edge of the room. "Have you been avoiding me? I haven't seen you since this morning."

"Not really." Rylie keeps working, hunched over the desk. "Just busy."

"Did you eat dinner?" Carriveau steps up behind her. "I didn't see you in the refectory."

"I made a sandwich."

Carriveau places her hands on Rylie's shoulders, intending to massage her, but Rylie tenses, holding a sharp draw of breath in her lungs, her pen frozen in the middle of a word, her discomfort apparent.

Rejected, Carriveau withdraws. "You've been shut away in here for hours." She pulls out a chair beside the teen. "What are you working on?"

"My suicide note."

The silence is painful.

Rylie stays focused on her notebook, waiting for an angry rebuke that never comes. Instead, she hears a strangled sob, the sound smothered by a hand pressed over a gasping mouth.

She tosses her pen down, whirling her chair around to find Carriveau in tears.

"I'm sorry." She wheels closer. "I didn't mean that." She grapples for Carriveau's hands, peeling them away from her trembling lips. "That was a shitty thing for me to say."

"*Pas de problème.* It's okay." Carriveau struggles to swallow, determined to regain her poise. "I think I probably deserve the sharp end of your tongue."

"No, you don't." Shamed by her careless disregard for Carriveau's feelings, Rylie almost comes to tears herself. "I don't want to hurt you."

She rolls back to her spot at the table and dumps the contents of her backpack out, spilling pens, pencils, tampons, a ruler, several erasers, two chocolate bars, an assortment of school books, her day planner, and ... a packet of tissues! She pulls one from the packet and trundles back to Carriveau, careful not to wheel over her feet.

"Here." She hands it over. "No more tears, else you'll set me off."

"*Merci, ma chérie.*" Carriveau wipes her eyes and blows her nose. "I've never cried in front of a student before."

"I'm not your student," Rylie contests. "At least, that's not *all* I am." She runs a hand over Carriveau's thigh. "I hope I mean more to you than that."

"Oh, Rylie, of course you do. I'm terrified of how you're making me feel, but that doesn't stop me from feeling it."

"I'll be careful with you, Vivienne, I promise." Rylie seeks out Carriveau's fingertips with her own, brushing skin against skin. "I know why you're so afraid, and that won't happen with me. I won't—" She stops herself.

Too late.

Carriveau knows precisely how that sentence would have ended, and more tears threaten to spill.

"You've found out about Kaitlyn, obviously."

Rylie nods.

"Who told you?" Carriveau sniffs.

"Adel."

The distressed Housemistress rolls her eyes. "Of course she did."

"Why is she such a bitch?"

"Rylie ..." Carriveau clutches her forehead, knowing she should chastise her pupil, but not really caring to. "Don't be rude."

"Why not? She *is* a bitch, and she acts like you belong to her. Did you know that?"

"She gets jealous," Carriveau dismisses it.

"I'd call it possessive."

"She's lonely."

"She's mental," Rylie counters. "She bloody clobbered me!"

In an instant, Carriveau's concern shifts entirely to Rylie, her own pain forgotten. "*She* did that to you?! Why wouldn't you tell me?"

Rylie winces, wishing she had better control of her mouth. "Please don't say anything to her; it's not worth it."

"But I—"

Rylie hushes Carriveau's objection before it fully forms. "You know it wouldn't help."

Pained by the reality of her impotence, Carriveau concedes that Rylie's right: any intervention on her part would likely have very few positive repercussions, and indeed, would more likely fuel Adel's animosity. In light of that, she turns her mind back to the reason she came looking for Rylie in the first place: she owes the teen an apology.

"Rylie, can we talk about last night?"

"Was it really an accident?" Rylie drives straight to the point.

Carriveau shakes her head. "I acted impulsively, but I knew what I was doing."

141

"You fucked me," Rylie presses on.

"I know." Carriveau's voice is barely above a whisper.

"Do you regret it?" Rylie forces herself to ask.

After a while, "*Oui.*"

Rylie tries to wheel away, but Carriveau grabs the arm of the chair and spins her back, forcing her to stay engaged, cupping her face to ensure eye contact.

"I shouldn't have fucked you," she explains. "You deserve better than a sneaky, clumsy, drunken late night tryst in the Lower Sixth dormitory. It was disrespectful of me to treat you that way."

"But what you do with Adel ... what you *used* to do with Adel ..."

Carriveau cringes, her cheeks reddening with embarrassment. "Did she tell you about that, too?"

"No, I saw you. On my first night here, I saw you standing outside the dormitory door."

"I've never touched her," Carriveau swears vehemently. "I've never done anything more than what you saw, and I haven't done that since I started ..."

She seems set to make a proclamation, but then changes her mind.

"You should get upstairs," she says instead. "I sent everyone else up before I came in here. It's past curfew."

Rylie nods, wheeling back to the table, clearing up her things.

Before she leaves, "I love you, Vivienne. I won't stop telling you."

She gives her reticent Housemistress a peck on the cheek before heading upstairs to the unusually silent Lower Sixth dormitory. As soon as she enters, she knows there's something amiss. Voices drop to whispers, then tail off completely, all eyes on her.

"What's going on?" she asks.

No-one answers.

She makes her way down the aisle toward her cubicle, waiting for the penny to drop. They couldn't possibly know that she was alone with Carriveau, could

142

they? Did someone eavesdrop? Has Adel said something? Why would she?

One more step.

And another.

And ... Rylie catches sight of something on her bedspread: a noose.

Cut from the spools of manila rope found backstage in the performance hall, it's been laid out most precisely, the knot expertly tied. It takes no great leap of imagination to make the connection: Kaitlyn must've hanged herself.

"Who did this?" Rylie drops her backpack at the foot of her cubicle, pivoting to lock her eyes on Adel. "*You* did this!"

She takes one step toward Adel, and Adel matches her. The two seem set to meet in the middle of the aisle, furies blazing, but a fuss kicks off. Girls from all sides—including Gabby—dart from their cubicles, keeping the two apart, squealing, shrieking, and yelling.

The noise draws Carriveau in.

"What's all this racket?" she demands sternly from the doorway.

The room falls silent.

Carriveau looks from left to right, from one startled pair of eyes to another, waiting for an explanation. When one isn't forthcoming, she strides into the room to commence her own investigation, but Rylie cuts her off, attempting to herd her away.

"It's all right." She puts her hands on Carriveau's shoulders. "I can take care of it."

Carriveau freezes, flashing Rylie a warning glare: Back off.

"Take care of what, Harcourt?"

Rylie withdraws her hands, but keeps the aisle barred to Carriveau. "You don't need to see this, Vivienne. Please."

At the sound of her first name on Rylie's lips, Carriveau, now visibly angered, clenches her jaw and pushes the defiant teen aside. Gabby dives for Rylie's cubicle to try and hide the noose, but she trips and falls at Carriveau's feet.

Carriveau steps over her, fixating on the morbid presentation. With the eyes of the entire Lower Sixth on her, she dare not cry; she dare not show weakness. Breathing heavily, exercising a remarkable amount of control, she turns from the cubicle and walks slowly back down the aisle, targeting Adel as she reaches the threshold of the room.

"Burn it," she growls, slamming the dormitory door on her way out.

CHAPTER THIRTEEN

RYLIE CAN'T GET COMFORTABLE. SHE TOSSES FROM left to right and back again, rolling with such force that she nearly throws herself out of bed on two occasions. Tormented by the thought of Carriveau locked in her private quarters, probably crying, alone, and in need of a friendly hand, sleep eludes her, her heart aching with sympathy for Carriveau's grief.

She's still awake when the sun rises, and she lies tucked in a ball, waiting for the melodious cadence of Carriveau's warm voice to sweep through the Lower Sixth dormitory, sticking steadfastly to routine as she knows she must.

But eight thirty comes and goes, and the dormitory remains silent. Groggy and tired, Rylie grapples for her phone on the bedside table, confirming the current time: eight forty-five.

Carriveau's never woken them up even a minute late, and now it's almost nine o'clock. Maybe she forgot to set her alarm. Maybe she slept badly, too. Maybe—

The dormitory door slams back on its hinges, an unfamiliar perfume drifting in, an irritable, curt voice rousing the Lower Sixth without care or feeling.

Rubbing her eyes, Rylie rolls onto her back, squinting at the frumpy figure making her way through the room: it's Miss Ansell.

"Up!" the geography teacher commands them harshly, banging on cubicle walls. "I can't have you rat-bags lying about in bed all day! Ups-a-daisy!"

Rylie is the last one to comply, vainly hoping that Carriveau may yet arrive to take over for her sullen Deputy, purring an apology in French before clapping her hands and ushering them all into the bathroom. Unfortunately, all she gets for her hesitation is a slap on the ankle.

"Get up!" Miss Ansell barks. "Lazybones!"

Though she's had next to nothing in the way of rest, Rylie drags herself out from the covers and stumbles with the others toward the bathroom, taking a long look at the closed and locked door to Carriveau's private rooms.

Clinging to the possibility that her always prompt and reliable Housemistress may simply not have had the heart to enter the dormitory so soon after last night's cruel stunt, she gets cleaned and dressed as quickly as she can—in neat but casual clothes, as is permitted on Sundays—and runs downstairs, determined to restore the light to those bright green eyes ... if she can find them.

The door to Carriveau's study is open, the room empty. She's not in the common room, nor in the kitchen, and her car isn't parked in its usual spot outside the house. Fearing something may be afoot, she resorts to talk to Miss Ansell, cornering her in the kitchen after breakfast.

"Where's Miss Carriveau?"

Miss Ansell fiddles with buttons on the dishwasher, squinting to see which ones to press, too busy working her way through Carriveau's morning chores as well as her own to give Rylie even a moment of her time.

"What Miss Carriveau does on her days off is none of your concern," she grumbles over her shoulder.

"Is she all right?" Rylie persists. "When will she be coming back?"

"Look"—Miss Ansell glares at her—"I don't know what your game is, but Miss Carriveau doesn't deserve all this nonsense. She's kind and affectionate, and you buggers are all the same: you take advantage of her." The irritated geography teacher gives the floor a cursory once-over with a horsehair broom. "Thankless takers, the whole bleeding lot of you."

Rylie shakes her head earnestly. "I wouldn't ever do anything to hurt her."

Miss Ansell snorts air through her nostrils, but doesn't comment.

"She is coming back, isn't she?" Rylie pushes her for answers.

Doing her best to ignore the teen, Miss Ansell carries about her business, first putting away the broom, then wiping down the tables. Undeterred, Rylie waits, grabbing Miss Ansell's arm when she tries to leave the room.

"Is Vivienne coming back?"

Caught off-guard by the child's impudence, Miss Ansell's first inclination to castigate Rylie for her behavior is abruptly dampened by the unexpectedly sincere look of concern in the teen's eyes, and it takes the short-tempered geography teacher a moment to gather her wits.

"She shouldn't, if she's got any bloody sense."

The older woman tears herself away, leaving Rylie alone, her fears unabated. A rumble of hunger gurgles in the pit of her stomach, but her heartache for Carriveau has her wound up in knots, and she takes no more than a bite of toast before she feels nauseous.

And she smells burning.

After ruling out the possibility that she's set fire to the brand new toaster, she follows the stink through the house to the back door, tracing it to an old barbecue on which Adel is burning the manila rope noose in the middle of a patch of grass that passes for a back garden.

She should walk away. She doesn't.

"Are you happy now? Is this what you wanted?" Rylie steps toward her, standing close enough that she can feel the heat from the fire. "Miss Carriveau's gone."

Adel stays silent, poking the burning rope with a spatula, turning it and rolling it like she's cooking a long sausage link, her eyes focused on the task.

"Why are you doing this to her? Why are you being so mean?" Rylie moves as near as she dares, the flames raging, licking furiously in all directions, twisting in time with the wind. "She doesn't love you."

Adel spins to face her—the white-hot spatula clenched so tightly in her hand that her knuckles turn pale with tension—and Rylie stumbles back a few paces, tripping over an old lacrosse stick and falling bum first into a pile of freshly mown grass.

Adel tosses the spatula onto the lawn, fuming. "Everything was fine until you came here," she snarls, strutting back into the house.

Alone again, Rylie picks greenery out of her hair, thankful that she'd taken herself down, however clumsily, before Adel had a chance to do it for her.

For the rest of the day, she makes a concerted effort to avoid the company of others—even Gabby—and grumps about in a mope, barely eating, even skipping a traditional Sunday roast in the refectory. Unable to concentrate on even the simplest task, her homework and her house chores go neglected, leading Miss Ansell to put a black mark in her student record for laziness.

Come bedtime, she has no intention of sleeping. She lies awake for several hours, listening for the rumble of a car engine, or the bang of the front door. When she feels herself drifting into slumber, exhaustion getting the better of her, she creeps out of bed and into the hall, settling resolutely in front of the door to Carriveau's rooms.

Must stay awake, she thinks to herself.

Must stay awake.

Must ... stay ... awake.

Must ... stay ...

In the wee hours of the morning, Carriveau turns the corner into the dimly lit Lower Sixth hallway and hesitates, spotting a crumpled bundle of blonde hair, pink skin, and white cotton lying limply at the door to her private quarters.

Stilettos clip-clopping on the floor, she steadily approaches the rhythmically heaving mass and crouches beside it, finding Rylie sound asleep, her head resting awkwardly against the door, her hair flopped in front of her face.

She's only wearing her short cotton nightdress, the hem bunched up around her hips, and it affords her little warmth. Her arms are hugged tightly around her midsection, trying to preserve as much body heat as possible, almost every bit of bare skin pricked with gooseflesh.

Carriveau extends a hand to wake her, brushing a thick lock of hair out of her eyes, tucking it behind her ear, startled to find her cold to the touch.

"Rylie," she purrs softly, to no effect.

For attempt number two, she lays a warm hand on Rylie's exposed ankle. "*Chérie*," she whispers against Rylie's ear, gliding her hand up the teen's smooth calf and thigh, edging beneath the hem of her nightdress.

Rylie's pale eyes flutter open, taking a moment to adjust, relieved to see Carriveau's familiar form before her.

"You came back!" She lunges forward, flinging her arms around Carriveau's neck with such force that she almost knocks the unprepared French woman off her feet.

Carriveau squeals, bracing herself against the wall. "Always so exuberant!"

Rylie buries her face in Carriveau's loose, dark tresses, inhaling her. "I missed you." She clutches fistfuls of Carriveau's hair, grabbing at any part of her that she can get her hands on. "I've been so worried about you."

"Sshhh." Carriveau soothes her, reaching up to unlock the door. "Come with me."

She helps Rylie onto her feet and leads her inside, setting her down upon the sofa, rubbing her chilly arms, trying to draw some warmth back.

"May I get you something to drink? Perhaps something with a little heat."

Rylie spies a bar fridge tucked under a table on the other side of the room. "What've you got? Are you hiding more booze in here?"

Carriveau sheds her suit jacket—leaving her in one of her standard skirt and blouse ensembles—and pulls a bottle of vodka from the freezer compartment in the fridge.

Rylie giggles. "You're awesome."

"I'm only giving you a tipple to warm you up," Carriveau warns, pouring a generous measure into a beaker she repurposed from the science lab. "I'm not getting you drunk."

She hands Rylie the beaker and sits beside her on the sofa, wrapping one arm around her shoulders, pressing the other to her chest, lightly squeezing her ribs.

Rylie winces. "Owie."

"Oops." Carriveau retracts her hand. "I forgot."

Rylie snuggles tighter, the beaker in her grasp, warmth radiating between them. "Don't apologize. I like having you close to me." She peers down at Carriveau's shoes, spying some dried dirt on the heels. "Where were you today?"

"What does it matter?" Carriveau kisses the side of Rylie's head, skirting around the subject of her whereabouts. "*Je suis ici maintenant.* I'm here now."

"I'm sorry. I'm not trying to pry." Rylie sips the vodka, screwing up her face, her first taste of unadulterated hard liquor burning her throat. "I was just afraid, that's all."

"Afraid?"

"That you wouldn't come back." Rylie braves another sip.

"Oh, darling. I wouldn't do that to you." Carriveau nuzzles her face into the teen's hair. "If it'll ease your mind to know, I went to visit Kaitlyn. It's a long drive, and that's why I was gone so long." She strokes Rylie's locks. "There was no need to fret."

Rylie glances again at the traces of dirt on Carriveau's shoes: cemetery dirt.

She takes another gulp of courage. "What Adel did—"

"I don't want to talk about it," Carriveau shuts her down. "Please."

"Are you in love with her?" Rylie downs the rest of the vodka, growing accustomed to the fire it brings with it. "Is that why you keep putting on the brakes when you're with me?"

Carriveau shakes her head. "I no more belong to Adel than I do to any of the other girls." She sets the empty beaker on the coffee table. "None of them have ever been alone with me in my private quarters. None of them have ever kissed me, or ... touched me. Nor I them."

"But Kaitlyn was different?"

Carriveau answers carefully, nodding. "Kaitlyn was different. *You're* different." She tightens her grip around Rylie's shoulders. "*Tu me rends faible.*"

Rylie recognizes the words: You make me weak.

That was one of Carriveau's first confessions, and she can't help but wonder if Kaitlyn made her weak, too. Is that what all this is about?

Clasping her hands in her lap, Rylie picks at a chip in one of her fingernails. "Do I remind you of her?"

"Yes," Carriveau answers honestly, stroking Rylie's golden hair, wishing she didn't see so much of Kaitlyn in her appearance.

151

"Is that why you like me?" Rylie keeps her eyes downturned. "You wish I was her?"

"No!" Carriveau answers emphatically, pressing a series of rapid woodpecker kisses all over her head and cheek, venturing toward her mouth. "I won't lie, that's why you caught my eye when I first saw you. It's why I couldn't take my eyes off you, and why my defenses dropped so easily around you, but that's as far as it goes." She tenders her young lover an Eskimo kiss. "It's *you* I'm attracted to, Rylie." She pulls the teen more deeply into her embrace. "It's *you* I spent hours with in my study, flirting and talking, having the most wicked thoughts, and becoming hopelessly, madly lost in you."

Twisting in her Housemistress's arms, Rylie strains her neck to make eye contact. "Will you tell me what happened between you and Kaitlyn?"

"*Pourquoi?*" Carriveau's grip relaxes.

"Because I want you to stop holding back." Rylie illustrates her point by clamping her hand over Carriveau's on her shoulder, coaxing firmness into her touch. "You pull away from me whenever her name is mentioned."

"I don't mean to." Carriveau caresses Rylie's cheek, exploring her face, preparing to relinquish the truth. "Kaitlyn loved me too much, and I let her. All I shouldn't have done, I did. I let my boundaries slip, and it was to her great detriment."

"You had an affair," Rylie reduces.

"It wasn't an affair." Carriveau's hand falls away. "Kaitlyn was ... a singular exception." She looks down at the loving girl in her arms. "Or so I thought. She was a transfer, just like you, except she was already eighteen. She'd been out of school since her GCSEs—entirely focused on sports—but when an injury forced her out of her last national competition, she enrolled here."

"You loved her?"

Carriveau nods, shaking a tear loose. "What Kaitlyn and I did wasn't illegal. Immoral, maybe, questionably, but not illegal. She wasn't even taking any of my classes." Looking down, she fidgets with the hem of Rylie's nightdress. "I assure you, the other girls at this school are nothing more than children to me. I've taught many of them since they were eleven or twelve years old."

Rylie does the sums: Carriveau's been working at Larkhill far longer than she's been a Housemistress.

"How long have you been stuck in this god awful place?"

"Since I was sixteen." Carriveau backhands the tear away, laughing sardonically at her own misfortune. "My parents sent me here to attend sixth form."

"And you never escaped?"

"I did, briefly. I graduated, went to university, got my master's degree, then came back." Carriveau sighs. "Though God only knows why." She stares up at the ceiling, as if the answer might be written up there in the cracked paintwork. "I taught all the way through my doctorate. Missus Bursnell made me the Head of Modern Languages, then gave me a Housemistress position. The more I thought about leaving, the more she anchored me here."

"That's flattering, isn't it?"

"It's my family's money she likes, not me. My parents have been benefactors of this school since I was first enrolled here." Carriveau focuses back on Rylie. "*Mais je m'éloigne*; I digress." She tucks the teen's hair behind her ears. "I want you to know that I don't look at *any* of my other students the way I look at you ... or the way I looked at Kaitlyn."

"What about Adel?"

"That isn't what you think it to be." Another tear escapes from Carriveau's shimmering emerald eyes. "After Kaitlyn died, she gave me an outlet for my grief."

"She took advantage of you?" Rylie catches the tear with her thumb.

Carriveau smiles appreciatively, reveling in Rylie's attentiveness. "She caught me in Kaitlyn's cubicle when I was packing up her things to send home to her parents. I thought I was alone in the house, so I was taking my time. She came into the dormitory and ... *comment dit-on?*" Carriveau endeavors to think of a delicate way to phrase it. "She touched herself in front of me." The saddened Housemistress covers her face, ashamed. "She must've overheard me and Kaitlyn having sex. She knew exactly how to mimic Kait's ..."

"It turned you on," Rylie concludes, sparing Carriveau from having to say it.

"If I closed my eyes, I could almost swear she was ..." Carriveau lets that sentence trail off. "Anyway, now there's you, *mon amour*, and Adel feels displaced. She'll be turning eighteen soon, and I think she's expecting ... well, you know."

Rylie strokes a hand up Carriveau's thigh, wriggling closer. "I know very well, and I can't blame her for wanting you." The hand moves higher up. "You're exquisite."

"I need to handle things with her." Carriveau tries to ignore the furtive hand. "I can't have her threatening you and hurting you."

The hand works its way up to her breast as Rylie starts nuzzling her neck, kissing and biting her, delving inside her blouse.

"Oh, Rylie. *Qu'est-ce que tu fais*? What're you doing?" Carriveau giggles. "Did that vodka go to your head?"

"I want you," Rylie whispers, dipping her hand inside Carriveau's bra, seeking out her nipple and pinching it, teasing it, making it hard. "All of you."

"I know you do." Carriveau whines, exercising all of her will power to pull Rylie's hand away. "But did anyone see you leave the dormitory?"

Rylie shakes her head, making a bid for re-entry into Carriveau's blouse.

"Are you sure?" Carriveau holds her at bay.

Rylie nods, drawing her into a kiss, knowing precisely what she's asking. "Adel's asleep."

In the midst of the kiss, Carriveau's grip on Rylie's hand relaxes, allowing the teen to dip back inside her bra, grabbing a handful of bare breast.

Her breathing quickens as Rylie's kisses drop lower, heading for her cleavage.

"Wait, Rylie." She hooks the teen's chin and tilts her head up. "I want to tell you something."

"What?" Rylie rubs noses with her.

Carriveau removes Rylie's hand from her bra for the second time. "*Je suis toute mouillée.*" She uncrosses her legs, kissing Rylie's fingers. "Do you know what that means?" She parts her legs and guides Rylie's hand up her skirt. "I'm so wet for you."

She's not exaggerating.

Rylie repositions for better leverage and dives inside her damp knickers, pushing two fingers inside her with one sure thrust, making her moan. The walls of her sex are swollen, her clit engorged with blood: she needs to come.

Rylie fingers her steadily, palming her clit, tapping and probing the most sensitive place within her, bringing her to the very edge of a powerful climax, then ... she withdraws.

Carriveau whimpers discontentedly, bucking her hips up toward the retreating fingers, trying to capture them and pull them back in, but Rylie resists.

"I want to taste you," she exclaims, sliding off the sofa.

Kneeling between Carriveau's legs, she grabs the hem of the lacy, sodden knickers and tugs them down, casting them off onto the sofa cushions. In full surrender, Carriveau wriggles her hips forward, spreading her legs wider and pulling up her skirt.

"You're the first since ..." She trembles slightly, baring the tops of her stockings and her milky thighs beyond. "There's been no-one else."

Understanding the enormity of that, Rylie slows her approach, taking her time to fully appreciate what's being offered to her. At the apex of Carriveau's thighs, the luscious folds of her sex are glistening with arousal, ready to be claimed, and Rylie brings both hands up, using her thumbs to tease those folds apart, baring the pink slit at the center.

"I love you," she whispers, trailing kisses up Carriveau's inner thighs, working her way toward the source of the intoxicating womanly scent filling her nostrils.

When she reaches her goal, she drops kisses on the small patch of wiry dark hair on Carriveau's mound, then slips lower, flicking her tongue below and around the swollen nub of her clit before moving lower still, probing her opening.

Carriveau fists Rylie's hair, pulling it back and out of her face, giving her an unrestricted view of the teen's bobbing head. She bites her lip, trying to be quiet, the only sound her labored, erratic breathing, but as she gets close to convulsing in her lover's mouth, she begins lose control, whimpering and mewling, her legs shaking.

She clutches the back of Rylie's head, hooking one leg over her shoulder, babbling some muttered French that Rylie has no need to translate, the meaning apparent when Carriveau suddenly yowls and comes.

Rylie doesn't resurface until Carriveau's orgasm has completely passed, her arms and legs relaxing their hold, her body going limp on the sofa. Even then, she stays where she is, resting her cheek on Carriveau's thigh, stroking her soft skin.

When Carriveau finally opens her eyes, she finds Rylie smiling up at her.

"I didn't hold back," she pants breathlessly. "I don't want to." She runs her thumb over Rylie's moist lips. "Not anymore."

"Please don't be afraid to love me." Rylie kisses her palm.

Leaning forward, Carriveau pulls Rylie up into a sex-flavored lip-lock. "Give me some time." Another kiss. "Be patient, *s'il te plaît*."

She's exhausted, barely able to keep her eyes open, and Rylie's not faring much better.

"I should get back to the dorm." The teen scrambles up off her knees. "I'll be able to sleep now that I know you're okay."

Carriveau lets her slip away. "*Bonne nuit, mon amour.*" She tosses a small ball of fabric at her departing lover.

Rylie catches the offering before it hits her in face: the drenched knickers.

"*Bonne nuit, Vivienne.*"

CHAPTER FOURTEEN

THE FOLLOWING MORNING, ORDER IS RESTORED. Carriveau strides into the Lower Sixth dormitory right on time, waking the girls with a cheerful smile and a burst of energy. By the time she gets to Rylie's cubicle, Rylie is kneeling on her bed, wide awake.

Feigning a yawn, Rylie stretches, lifting her arms high over her head, causing the hem of her short nightdress to rise above her crotch, revealing her lacy knickers. Or rather, Carriveau's lacy knickers.

"*Bonjour.*" Carriveau feasts on the sight. "Sleep well?"

"*Oui.*" Rylie beams. "*Et toi?*"

"Exceedingly." Carriveau scarcely pauses on her arc, continuing her circuit of the room. "Today, we start afresh." Her eyes fall briefly upon Adel.

Before her mood has a chance to sour, she glances back at Rylie, witnessing a thunk and a flail of arms and legs as the overly eager teen leaps out of bed too fast, catches her foot in the duvet, and face-plants on the floor.

"I see I'm not the only one who's hungry to get this brand new day underway." Carriveau chuckles, retracing her steps, peering down on Rylie, lying half in and half out of her cubicle. "Are you hurt?" She offers her hand.

"P'raps she needs the kiss of life, Miss!" Gabby heckles her from the neighboring cubicle, leaning over the dividing wall with a goofy grin.

Ignoring the taunt, Rylie accepts Carriveau's help with one hand, the other pressed to her ribs. "I'm fine," she croaks. "Never better."

"Nothing a good breakfast won't fix." Carriveau harnesses her green eyes to Rylie's blues. "When you're ready."

Rylie receives the message loud and clear: If you hurry, we might be able to steal a few minutes alone.

To that end, she gets a wriggle on and makes it down to the kitchen in seven and a half minutes flat, arriving to find Carriveau standing at the counter, licking jam off her fingers.

"*Pour toi, ma chérie.*" Carriveau pushes a plate of toast toward her, the slices already laden with jam, and puts a finger to her lips, indicating secrecy.

"*Merci, Vivienne.*" Rylie greets her *en français*, kissing one cheek then the other, both hands on her waist.

"I can't stay." Carriveau pinches Rylie's lips between her own, murmuring softly as she feels Rylie's hands slip down to caress her bum. "I have to leave early for a senior staff meeting."

"Can I have you for a few minutes in your study?" Rylie coaxes her into another smooch.

"Mmm, if only." Carriveau breaks the kiss and checks her watch. "But I must go. That means Miss Ansell will be doing the uniform inspections this morning." She slithers free. "Try not to get as carried away with her as you do with me." She winks.

As other Upper and Lower Sixth girls start to spill into the kitchen, Carriveau makes her way out, heading for the main school building. Much to her displeasure, she's about to spend the next forty minutes stuck in a stuffy boardroom, the carpet covered with coffee stains, the walls decorated with portraits of Headmistresses past, the antique mahogany table riddled with chewing gum on its underside.

160

Five minutes in, she's bored. After thirty more minutes, she's positively sick to death of listening to Missus Bursnell prattle on about matters of little importance: arranging for someone to come and polish the weather vane; repainting the lines on the hockey field; replacing the chocolate in the vending machine with granola bars and rice crackers; and decreasing kitchen costs by cutting back on "Frivolous cake-making."

At that, Carriveau struggles to stifle a laugh.

"Yes, Vivienne?" Missus Bursnell gripes at her. "Is there something you'd like to say?"

Carriveau holds up her hand, signaling no, and shares a smile with another younger Housemistress on the other side of the table. They're the only two Housemistresses under the age of forty, and often find themselves close allies in matters of school policy.

"Very well." Missus Bursnell shuffles papers. "Then if there's no further business—"

Around the table, Housemistresses and heads of department begin to rise.

"*En fait*"—Carriveau speaks up then, raising her hand—"*une chose de plus.*"

Missus Bursnell sighs. "Is it too much to ask that you speak English when you're convened with us, Vivienne? This isn't the modern languages department."

As Miss Ansell has a tendency to do, Missus Bursnell treats Carriveau's name with added harshness when she's irritated, making the docile French woman instantly testy.

"I want to discuss the upcoming sixth form concert we have planned for our generous financial donors." Carriveau waits until everyone is reseated before she continues. "I thought we could open up the performance hall."

The room falls silent.

"So soon?" one of the other Housemistresses asks after a heavy pause, scratching at her gray bob of hair with the eraser end of a pencil.

161

"Soon?" Carriveau raises an eyebrow. "It's been almost a year. What else are we going to do? Let it fall into a state of disrepair? It seems silly not to utilize the full resources we have at our disposal." She turns to Missus Bursnell. "I think the school's ready to forge ahead, *non?*"

"And you?" Missus Bursnell turns the question back on her.

"Don't pretend that you care." Carriveau eyes her with a healthy dose of disdain. "Are you allowing us to use the performance hall, or not?"

The older woman nods slowly. "If that's your wish, I have no objection, but how will you get it ready in time? The concert's on Friday, and tomorrow most of the sixth form will be away on a trip. They won't be back until Wednesday evening, and they'll need Thursday free for final rehearsals."

Carriveau shrugs, unfazed. "I can gather up some volunteers and have the task finished this evening, if you'll permit me to keep one or two of the girls up past their curfew."

"What's wrong with the hall we've been using all this time?" the head of the drama department protests.

"It's an old gym hall with a temporary stage built in it. It's a relic from before the new sports building was erected." The younger Housemistress sides with Carriveau. "It's really not appropriate."

Missus Bursnell rolls her eye, the glass one veering ever further leftward. "So be it." She makes a note in one of her many jotters. "Any other brilliant ideas, Vivienne?" She asks the question sarcastically, not expecting a response.

Carriveau soldiers on.

"I also thought some of the students enrolled in the after-class music club could be invited to perform this time." She turns her attention to the head of the music department. "I'm sure you have a few sixth form pupils who might appreciate the opportunity for inclusion. Especially since they're so often overlooked in favor of those enrolled in your A-level programs, despite the fact that many of them display an equal or greater musical talent."

"I take it you're referring to the Harcourt child you forced upon me?"

Carriveau smiles innocently. "If you think she's good enough."

The music teacher waves a flippant hand, not giving too much of a shit one way or the other. "As it happens, one of my soloists just came down with laryngitis. Harcourt may fill her spot." She leans back in her chair, stretching. "It makes no difference to me."

"It's settled then," the Headmistress proclaims. "And Miss Carriveau," she says, before the French woman has a chance to get up out of her chair, "you shall be in charge."

That suits Carriveau just fine, and she sets the caretakers to work right away, removing the 'Do Not Enter' signs and giving the place a vigorous dusting. She's standing in the main doorway, watching them clean the red velvet curtains hanging from the proscenium arch above the stage, when Rylie nudges up beside her, bumping her shoulder.

"I've just been asked to perform at the concert on Friday night." She stands close to Carriveau, even the slight contact of their shoulders feeling dangerously illicit. "Did you do this?" She nods to the performance hall.

"No, not really." Carriveau sighs, staring wistfully into the hall. "You did."

"How?" Rylie frowns. "What did I do?"

"You make me happy, Rylie. Happier than I've been in a long time." Carriveau feels out Rylie's hand between them, touching her fingers softly, not daring to be so reckless as to properly hold her hand. "This school needs to move on, and so do I." She pulls back, too afraid to let the intimacy linger. "You made that clear to me last night."

"I'll make it even clearer to you tonight, if you'll let me."

"Tonight?" Carriveau's red lips curl upward. "Tonight, I'll be looking for volunteers to help me get the performance hall ready. I can't promise that there'll be a chance for anything more than a bit of light flirtation, but it will mean the opportunity to stay up past curfew if you want to come by and lend a hand after your evening study hour."

"What will you be wearing?"

"Is that what it depends upon?" Carriveau smirks.

"Every little helps."

Rylie catches Carriveau's eye as she enters the backstage area of the performance hall after rushing through her homework. Carriveau, whose last class ended at two o'clock, has been here for most of the afternoon and evening, and now she's balanced precariously on a chair, paintbrush in hand, decorating a ten foot high set piece that'll form part of the backdrop for one of the more elaborate songs being performed at the concert.

Other volunteers, at Carriveau's instruction, are clearing out the dump of props at the back of the hall, disposing of anything broken and sorting the old costumes into piles according to whether or not they're useful, utter rubbish, or in need of mending. Meanwhile, in the wings, one or two drama students are getting to grips with the lighting, and several more are trying to master the sound system.

Footsteps up above—rubber-soled boots stomping over metal walkways—reveal more pupils, changing the gel covers on the lights, adjusting things here and there. One of them whistles down to Rylie, hanging her head over one of the platforms.

It's Gabby.

Once she has Rylie's attention, she tips her head in Carriveau's direction, hinting in no uncertain terms that Rylie ought to nab this opportunity to approach their silently working Housemistress while she's by herself. Then, she holds both hands in front of her chest, jiggling a pair of enormous, imaginary breasts, thus demonstrating the universally accepted sign language for: "That gorgeous woman's showing off her phenomenal rack." Or more colloquially: "Have a look at the tits on that!"

Flicking her a vee—pasting on a scowl to go with it—Rylie turns away from Gabby and goes to Carriveau's aid. Her Housemistress is now at risk of toppling the chair as she strains to reach the very edge of the set piece—a problem that would be easily solved by getting down off the chair and moving it two feet to the left.

"Do you need help, *Mademoiselle*?"

Rylie positions herself in the perfect place for Carriveau to lean on her shoulder. In doing so, she gets an eyeful of Carriveau's abundant cleavage. Wearing a light cotton shirt, half unbuttoned, revealing a skintight camisole beneath, the generously proportioned Housemistress is unabashedly flaunting herself.

Rylie puts a hand on her jeans-covered thigh. "I don't want you to fall."

"Is that why you finally came over here?" Carriveau arches her back, making sure Rylie gets the best view of her assets. "You were concerned for my safety?"

"You looked like you could use a hand." Rylie gives Carriveau a squeeze, surreptitiously fondling her.

"*Ah bon?*" Carriveau deliberately overextends her reach, leaning further forward, tipping the chair and emitting a girlish squeal.

Rylie catches her and rights the chair, planting both hands firmly on her hips. "Perhaps two hands are better than one."

"Indeed." Carriveau drops the paintbrush to the floor, redirecting her free hand to Rylie's other shoulder, their faces just inches apart as she steps down off the chair.

The closeness lingers until she spies Adel entering the performance hall, forcing her to withdraw to a more appropriate distance.

"Are you excited for the concert on Friday?" She changes the subject.

"I'm not sure." Rylie eyes the piano with some hesitation. "I've never performed in front of an audience before."

"I've heard that you're supposed to imagine your audience *déshabillée, non*? That is to say, naked. Might that help?"

"Well, I'll be singing to you, and I already do that." Rylie pins her eyes to Carriveau's chest, marveling at the deep valley generated by her push-up bra, watching the upper swells of her breasts rise and fall with the rhythm of her breathing.

"Do you want to practice?" Carriveau lets her enjoy the sight for a few more seconds, then spins her toward the piano, giving her *derrière* a light shove. "Why don't you play me the song you intend to perform on Friday?"

Torn between running for the bathroom and succumbing to the lure of the ivories, the desire to please Carriveau eventually wins out above all else, and she takes her place at the grand instrument—albeit with great reluctance.

After three false starts, she gets past the eighth bar and hits her stride, only striking five wrong notes from the beginning to the end of a love song she wrote with one particular woman in mind: Carriveau.

Throughout, Carriveau is standing in the wings, smiling, blushing, swooning, blissfully unaware that Adel's standing not far behind her, glowering. Before the last note dies away, Gabby thunders down from the rigging and budges onto the piano stool next to Rylie, making the young musician smack down on the keys, causing a cacophonous din.

"That was brave!"

"No, it wasn't." Rylie covers the delicate keys with the fallboard, preventing another accident. "There's only, like, ten people here, and half of them weren't listening."

"Not that, I mean ..." Gabby looks around, shying away from Adel's glare. "Your song was about Miss Carriveau, yeah?" She drops her voice. "The last girl who publicly professed her love for Miss Carriveau ended up hanging from ..." She turns her eyes up to the rigging, then back down to Rylie.

The last girl? Kaitlyn, obviously.

"Why did she do it?" Rylie asks quietly, not sure if she really wants to know.

"Miss Carriveau denied the whole lot of it, and Kaitlyn couldn't take being rejected like that. People were calling her a liar, saying she was only after the attention and whatnot. Missus Bursnell said she had mental problems."

At that moment, the pupils who've been diligently putting together a playlist for the intermission music call it a night, leaving their laptop still hooked up to the sound system. A minute later, Adel's voice booms over the loud speakers, dedicating the next song to Miss Carriveau, then Britney Spears' Womanizer blares out.

Carriveau's mood takes a nosedive.

"Shut it off!" she barks with an extraordinary degree of hostility. "*Tout de suite!*"

"What's the matter?" Adel complies. "You don't like it?" She cues up a different song. "How about this instead?" She hits the play button, unleashing the chorus of Lily Allen's Fuck You.

In response to that, Carriveau marches over, yanks the plug on the music, grabs Adel by the elbow, and hauls the unruly teen out of the performance hall.

"Get back to the house! And go straight to the dormitory. I don't want to see hide nor hair of you again tonight."

"Really?" Adel feigns confusion. "You don't want me to wait up for you so that you can frig yourself while I—"

Carriveau slams the door on her.

In the silence that follows, she presses her back against the wall, battling to control her breathing. From left to right, all around the room, she feels her students' eyes burning into her. She can see their confusion, their concern, and perceives their judgment.

She can't bear it.

"*Ça suffit pour ce soir.*" She wipes away a stray tear, declaring their work here is done for the night. "Go back to your houses."

No-one moves.

"Now!" She slaps her open palm on the wooden paneling on the wall beside her to emphasize the order, making several of the girls jump before scurrying from the room.

All except Rylie.

Taking a chance that the instruction doesn't apply to her, Rylie moves steadily closer as Carriveau fumbles her cell phone out of her pocket and makes a call to Miss Ansell.

"Edwards is on her way back to the house," she informs her Deputy, allowing Rylie to approach her. "See to it that she goes straight up to the dormitory when she gets there. Laurenson's not far behind her."

On the other end of the phone, Miss Ansell enquires about the only other student from the house who's yet to return.

"Harcourt's with me." Carriveau fingers Rylie's hair, her mood softening, her anger and sadness abating. "I'm not sure when we'll be back. It could be a late night." She hangs up.

Rylie checks her watch: it's barely eight thirty.

"A late night, huh?" She creeps her hands around Carriveau's waist. "So what shall we do now?" She helps herself to Carriveau's lips. "Now that we're alone."

168

"What do you think we should do?" Carriveau wraps her fingers around the collar of Rylie's school shirt, holding on tight to her as she accepts another kiss. "Bearing in mind that, until you're eighteen, a love like this is illegal. We ought to behave."

That's the first time Rylie's ever heard her use the word love in a complete sentence. Sure, it's not quite a declaration, but it's damn close.

"I hope you're teasing." She strokes Carriveau's waist. "If you said you wanted to press pause on this now, I'm not sure I could comply. Not after last night."

She plays it down, but truthfully, she knows she wouldn't be able to back away from Carriveau's physical affections any more than she could turn from a slice of her favorite cake. It's too irresistible: the sight of it ... the smell of it ... the taste of it.

Coming to the same conclusion, Carriveau takes Rylie by the hand and leads her backstage, pausing briefly to glance up at the rigging.

"What're you looking at?" Rylie plays dumb.

"It's nothing." Carriveau shakes her head, slaps on a smile, and tugs Rylie down a dimly lit passage toward the dressing rooms.

She flings open the last door and steps into a tiny room filled with one of the piles of discarded costumes, all lazily dumped over the floor. The only light is one singular bulb around the dressing room mirror, the others either missing, burnt out, or broken.

"We can do as much or as little as you'd like," she says, letting down her hair and lowering herself onto the pile. "I'm content just to be alone with you."

She leans on her elbow, propping her head up on the heel of her palm, waiting to be joined by her lover, wanting only to feel the warmth of another body lying next to hers, their arms and legs entwined in an embrace.

Wanting distinctly more than that, and with as much calm deliberation as she can muster, Rylie shakes her own hair out, then sheds her ugly Larkhill cardigan ... and then the shirt beneath it ... and then the bra beneath that, leaving her topless, soon shivering against the cold.

"I'll warm you," Carriveau offers, welcoming her onto the makeshift bed.

As soon as Rylie's on her back, Carriveau begins trailing her fingertips over the teen's skin, around her breasts, down to her stomach, and back again, letting her fingernails drag, leaving goose bumps in their wake.

"You're so beautiful." She takes her time admiring Rylie's body. *"Très, très belle."*

Minutes pass.

When she's had her fill of ogling, she maneuvers on top of her young lover, sharing her body heat, mashing their breasts together, careful not to place any pressure on Rylie's bruised ribs. In this position, she reaches between them and delves a hand up Rylie's school skirt, finding that the mere anticipation of sex has her drenched.

Tendering smooches aplenty, she tickles Rylie's cunt with her fingertips, teasing the teen with faint caresses. "There's something I haven't done for you yet," she whispers, flicking her tongue against Rylie's ear before laying a kiss there.

Putting that mouth to good use, she begins kissing down Rylie's body, working her way between those alabaster thighs ... and then ...

Her phone starts ringing.

Carriveau blows her hair upwards out of her face and rises from Rylie's crotch, checking the call display. "It's Miss Ansell." She shuffles up Rylie's body, settling above her. "I must answer." She puts a finger to Rylie's lips, preventing a protest and ensuring silence as she takes the call, which proves to be short and sharp.

There's an annoyed "What?" followed by a "Still?" and a string of muttered French expletives. It ends with "I'll deal with it," and she hangs up.

"Adel?" Rylie guesses.

Carriveau nods. "She didn't go back to the house."

"So what do you have to do?"

"Find her." Carriveau scrambles up off the fabric. "I am still the Housemistress after all." She straightens her clothes. *"Pour le moment."*

For the time being? Rylie would question her on that off-hand comment, but Carriveau barely pauses to draw breath before she dives into another thought.

"Not to worry." She scoops Rylie's clothes off the floor, helping to dress her. "We're about to have almost two full days together." She buttons Rylie's shirt. "The other girls are leaving tomorrow morning on an overnight trip."

"Not me?"

"Nope." Carriveau pulls the cardigan around her shoulders. "You joined the school too late." She yanks Rylie in for a kiss. "I'll have you all to myself."

As it turns out, they need not have cut their intimacy short. By the time they get back to the house—where Carriveau gathers the girls in the kitchen, intending to question them on Adel's last known whereabouts—Adel's already there. Miss Ansell is in the midst of apologizing profusely for needlessly drawing Carriveau away from her work in the performance hall when Adel snorts and laughs.

"Work? Miss Carriveau sent all the volunteers away ages ago." She scowls at her arch nemesis. "She was alone with Rylie Harcourt."

Silence drops.

Looks are exchanged among the students, Miss Ansell shifts uncomfortably in the corner, keeping her lips tightly buttoned, and Carriveau takes a deep breath, refusing to crack.

"I want everyone up to the dormitories immediately," she says coolly, expecting compliance.

"But it's only nine thirty!" one of the Upper Sixth girls dares to grumble.

"Allez! Go," Carriveau barks. "This instant."

"Come on, girls," Miss Ansell rallies them, herding them out. "You heard her."

Adel is one of the last to get a move on, attempting to push between Carriveau and Rylie on her way out of the room.

"Not you." Carriveau holds her back. "Collect your overnight things and check yourself in to one of the seclusion rooms. After that stunt you pulled in the performance hall, and your unapologetically poor attitude, you're not welcome in this house tonight."

Adel tugs herself free. "Fine!" She stomps up the staircase, thundering into the dormitory.

Rylie hangs back, wary of getting in her way. "Where are you sending her?"

"We have a seclusion ward in the main school building," Carriveau explains, her arms folded, her expression grim. "A student may be excluded from her house for up to forty-eight hours as a punishment for antisocial behavior."

"What about the sixth form trip tomorrow? Will she be gated? Prohibited from going?"

Carriveau shakes her head, massaging her temple, a headache blossoming. "That'd be within my rights, but no. *Je ne veux pas d'elle ici.*"

She hides her true feelings behind the softly spoken French: I don't want her here.

"In the morning, Edwards will be rousted by the matron on duty," she goes on. "The coach driver will pick her up from the main building, along with all the other sixth form naughties, if there are any." She gives Rylie a light nudge. "Now you get upstairs with the others."

Disinclined to end the night on such a miserable note, Rylie lingers. Risking a telling off, she places a hand on the small of Carriveau's back, rubbing gently, and presses a peck on her cheek. She chances more—makes a bid for lips—but Carriveau turns away, indicating 'no' with a subdued shake of her head.

Adel stomps back down the staircase a few seconds later, her arms laden with nightclothes and toiletries. In the doorway, she stops, looking over her shoulder at Carriveau.

"Fuck you!" she yells loud enough for the whole house to hear, then slams the door on her way out.

CHAPTER FIFTEEN

RYLIE SETS HER OWN ALARM AND WAKES UP HALF an hour before Carriveau is due to do her morning rise-and-shines. Having slept in her clothes to save time, she rolls out of bed, wrangles her hair, and makes a quick stop in the bathroom to brush her teeth before going on a hunt for her Housemistress.

She expects to find the usually predictable French woman in her study, gathering up her things for the day ahead, but she appears to have broken with routine this morning. She's not anywhere to be found, but the kitchen smells like freshly brewed coffee, betraying her recent presence there. Rylie can't hear any movement, but the faint stench of cigarette smoke is drifting in through an open window.

Following her nose, Rylie steps quietly into the laundry room and sneaks up to the back door, flinging it open with a playful "Boo!"

Carriveau, sitting on the back step, leaning against the door, nearly falls backwards onto Rylie's legs. After emitting a muted shriek, she rights herself and makes a weak effort to hide the cigarette she's holding, simultaneously brushing a packet of cigarettes and lighter off the top step and onto the one below, knocking them into an empty coffee mug that she's using as an ashtray, moving them out of sight. Only then does she look up and see that it's Rylie.

"*Dieu merci!*" She relaxes, fishing the cigarettes and lighter out of the mug. "I was afraid you were Miss Ansell," she mumbles, pinching the cigarette between her lips.

Rylie takes pause to enjoy this moment. For once in her life, she wasn't the one hurriedly extinguishing a cigarette and struggling to dispose of the evidence.

"Are you all right?" She closes the door and sits next to Carriveau on the step, feeling the chill of the concrete going straight through to her bones. "I didn't know you smoked."

"I don't." Carriveau blows a lungful of smoke into the crisp morning air.

"Neither do I." Rylie takes the cigarette from her, finding the ring of her red lipstick around the filter oddly sexy, the sensation only amplified—becoming borderline erotic—when she puts her own lips to the cigarette, feeling the tacky residue of the crimson paste transferring onto her baby pink mouth.

Reaching between them to tip ash into the makeshift ashtray Carriveau had so pointlessly tried to conceal, she notices the cigarette packet and lighter, recognizing them immediately.

"Wait a minute, are these the ciggies you confiscated from Gabby?" She laughs.

Carriveau doesn't bother to deny it. "You'd be surprised how much contraband gets snatched up by the faculty." She nabs her cigarette back. "You students always think you're so hard done by, but the rules apply to us just as they apply to you: no alcohol or cigarettes on school premises, no public displays of affection, the conservative dress code."

Rylie flashes her a cocked eyebrow.

"I take some liberties with that one," Carriveau admits, tugging on the hem of her mid-thigh length skirt. "Missus Bursnell disapproves, of course, but ... *je m'en fous.*"

176

Rylie frowns, the meaning lost on her. "*Qu'est-ce que tu as dit?*" she asks, needing a translation on this rare occasion.

Carriveau draws more poison into her lungs. "That's something you don't learn in the classroom, huh? How to curse." She passes the cigarette back to Rylie. "*Je m'en fous*: I don't give a fuck."

"*Je m'en fous,*" Rylie repeats, trying it on for size. "I like it. Will you teach me how to talk dirty to you in French? I know a few things, but I want to know more." She slides her hand over Carriveau's thigh, scrunching up the yielding Housemistress's skirt till the top of her stocking is bared. "I want to *do* more."

"Mmm." Carriveau leans back, resting her head against the door, her eyes closed. "If only we had the time. I have to be upstairs in"—she checks her watch—"ten minutes."

Despite her words, she lets Rylie wriggle a hand all the way between her legs, accepting the cigarette as it's passed back to her.

"I'm such a dreadful teacher."

"No, you're not." Rylie presses her middle finger into the cleft of Carriveau's sex, over her underwear, teasing her puffy labia.

"Says the student who's sharing a cigarette with me, and stroking my obscenely wet pussy behind the schoolhouse." Carriveau chuckles. "Yeah, you're right: I'm the very picture of propriety and discipline."

Rylie repositions to give herself a better angle for groping, but Carriveau staves her off, thwarting her attempt at penetration.

"Please don't." She finishes the cigarette, crushing it in the mug. "We'll have almost the whole day together, so there's no need to rush." She fishes Rylie's hand out from between her legs. "There'll be plenty of time for intimacy."

"I don't have classes?"

"Not normal ones. You can use this day to catch up on your French coursework while I teach my other classes."

Rylie pouts. "Lame."

"None of that." Carriveau gets up off the step and dusts herself down, secreting the contraband in her jacket pocket. "Unfortunately for us both, no matter what else you are, you're still my student, and one of many at that."

She clutches the mug in her hand and reaches for the door handle, but Rylie leaps up off the concrete and stops her.

"*Puis-je t'embrasser*?" she asks with doe eyes.

Unable to resist such a polite request for a kiss, Carriveau gives her one: a loving caress of tongues, meshing toothpaste, coffee, and cigarettes.

"Now that's it until you finish your homework," she says when it breaks, and they slip silently back into the house.

"Have you thought about what you're going to do with Adel?" Rylie asks, starting work on her breakfast while Carriveau washes out the mug.

"Believe me, I've thought of nothing else." The Housemistress sighs, banishing the mug to the dishwasher. "I've been very careless."

"Well, I'm not worried about her." Rylie slaps two pieces of bread in the toaster. "She's a bully, that's all. She won't get to me."

"You might not be worried about her, but *I* am. I have to be." Carriveau stands behind Rylie, rubbing her shoulders. "You're my responsibility—*all* of you. I can't disregard her feelings just because I've fallen—" She stops herself, the movement of her hands ceasing as abruptly as her words.

Rylie moves the conversation along, letting her off the hook, freeing her from the confession she's obviously still not ready to make.

"You wanna know something? I don't think she deserves your consideration."

"I did this to her. If she's a vindictive little shit, it's because of me." Carriveau consults her watch again. "I have to go."

Rylie doesn't try to hold her back. Her toast pops, and she slathers it with jam, taking a seat at one of the smaller tables, glad that she was able to get to the last loaf of white bread before some other student could finish it off, leaving her with the dreaded heels.

She's already halfway through by the time the first girls rush into the kitchen to grab a quick bite to eat before the coach arrives to whisk them away—Gabby among them.

"Don't do anything I wouldn't do!" She giggles, snatching a piece of toast off Rylie's plate. "All alone with our house mum. All night."

"Yeah, yeah, yeah." Rylie gives up the rest of her breakfast. "I'm going to be doing French coursework all day by the sounds of it. Lucky ole me."

While she continues to receive a pep talk from her best friend, Carriveau is in her study, receiving the opposite lecture from Miss Ansell.

"We can trade places if you like," the geography teacher offers. "You can go with the kiddies as a chaperone, and I'll stay here with whatsherface."

Carriveau, seated at her desk, filling out paperwork, looks up at Miss Ansell over the top of her reading glasses. "Why ever would I want you to do that?"

The two lock eyes.

Miss Ansell backs down first. "Fine, I give up." She flails her hands in the air. "All I will say is this: If you haven't done it already, don't." She pauses for emphasis. "The girl's not Kaitlyn."

Deeming it pointless to continue flogging this long dead horse, Miss Ansell shakes her head in resignation and walks off, seeing to the boarding of the coach in a firm and orderly manner. When the house falls quiet, Rylie peeks her head into Carriveau's study.

"I won't be a nuisance today, I promise."

"Nuisance, no." Carriveau sets down her pen. "Distraction, yes."

"When will you be done teaching?"

"I have five consecutive periods today, so I'll be back at the house by two thirty."

"Okay." Rylie's cogs whir. "And what will my reward be if I finish all my homework by then?"

Contemplating all the fun they're about to have with one another, Carriveau's mouth curls into the most delicious smile.

The echoes of Rylie's orgasm can be heard up and down the house, her release coming swiftly and powerfully. When it's over, Carriveau surfaces from beneath the covers, her hair tousled and unkempt, Rylie's fingers still tangled up in it.

"Was that worth waiting for?" She brings her mouth to Rylie's breasts, kissing her lover all over before rolling off her and onto the other side of the bed. "It's been so long since I've had the pleasure of a woman in my bed." She licks her lips, savoring the taste of Rylie's sex.

Rylie pants, relishing the last few contractions of her climax, writhing under the covers, bursting into a giggle. "I can't believe I'm *in* your bed."

She looks around the room, taking in the details for the first time. Carriveau has tomorrow's suit hanging on the dresser door, half a dozen silk scarves are draped over the bedroom mirror, a dresser is topped with makeup and nail polish, and a collection of stiletto-heeled shoes are lined up against one wall.

There are a few pictures here and there: Carriveau with an older couple who must be her parents, Carriveau with friends—possibly ex-girlfriends—and one picture of Carriveau with Kaitlyn. The latter is in a heart-shaped frame on the bedside table.

Rylie doesn't get a chance to fixate on it for long. Carriveau flings back the covers, casting her eyes over the teen's naked body, exposing her own nakedness at the same time.

She runs a hand from Rylie's shoulders over her breasts, her ribs, her waist, her flat stomach, and the mound of her sex.

"You're so soft." She drags her fingers through Rylie's pubic hair, toying with the barbell piercing below. "Does the piercing do anything for you?" she wonders, examining it.

Rylie looks down at herself, the silver jewelry shimmering with her own fluids and Carriveau's saliva. "It rubs against my clit when I'm turned on and my little button's all swollen."

Carriveau flicks it, eliciting another giggle.

"Careful." Rylie slaps her hand away, grinning. "It's sensitive." She pushes Carriveau onto her back, attacking her with kisses.

"Such exuberance!" Carriveau forces Rylie to break for air.

"I have to be exuberant." Rylie leans on the pillow, stroking Carriveau's face. "I never know when we're going to get time together, and I don't want to waste it."

Carriveau cups Rylie's cheeks, pulling her in for another kiss. "I wish this was easier."

"It's okay." Rylie snuggles up next to her. "I know how it has to be."

Carriveau cocks her head. "Have you done this before?" A curious smile starts to blossom on her lips. "Be truthful. I'm not your first teacher, am I?"

"You're my first French teacher."

Carriveau laughs heartily. "I should've known. You had no qualms about pursuing me. You knew well what you were doing, and you took it all in your stride." She rolls onto her side, pressing more tightly against Rylie. "Does this have anything to do with why you transferred schools so suddenly?"

"Maybe."

"What happened?" Carriveau prods her. "Please tell me nobody went to prison."

"Nobody went to prison." Rylie giggles. "My parents wouldn't stand for it. The shame a scandal like that would cause my family would be intolerable for them, so they'd much rather make you sign a non-disclosure agreement, pay you off, and send you somewhere far, far away."

"That's Missus Bursnell's attitude to a tee." Carriveau swings her leg over Rylie's hip, their arms and legs becoming further entangled. "So am I to assume that was the fate that befell my predecessor? What kind of teacher was she?"

"German, but technically, she was never my teacher. She taught at the sixth form college, and I was still taking my GCSEs at the secondary school on the adjoining campus when we met. So I wasn't doing it to get good grades or anything, and when I started at the sixth form, I didn't even take German. There was no conflict of interest."

"You must have a fetish for language teachers." Carriveau chuckles. "Did you love her?"

"Yes," Rylie answers solemnly.

"Was she your first?"

"Uh-huh. She took my virginity when I was fifteen."

"Ooh." Carriveau winces. "That was dreadfully naughty of her. How old was she?"

"She'd just turned thirty. I reckon she was having some kind of crisis brought on by the departure of her twenties, and being with me made her feel good about herself."

"I bet it did! You were half her age! Having said that, if you were living in France, she'd not have been breaking the law—age of consent there is fifteen. The divide of right and wrong in these matters can be so arbitrary. Were I not your teacher now, I'd not be breaking the law either."

"I'll be eighteen in six months, then we won't have to worry."

182

Carriveau regards her carefully, inspecting her fresh young face, tracing a finger over her smooth cheeks and full pink lips. "Have you always been attracted to older women?"

Rylie nods. "Mm-hmm, but you're not *that* much older than me. There's only"—she counts on her fingers—"fourteen years between us."

Carriveau laughs. "Only!"

"Why does it matter, anyway?" Rylie surprises her with a kiss, tasting herself on Carriveau's lips. "Who cares?"

"Your parents probably." Carriveau nuzzles Rylie's nose. "So tell me more about your ex-girlfriend. Was she beautiful?"

"Not a patch on you."

Carriveau murmurs noncommittally, twirling a lock of Rylie's hair around her finger. "I suppose you have to say that, since you're naked in my bed."

"I'm not lying!" Rylie wriggles to the edge of the bed, leans over, and fishes her cell phone from the pocket of her doffed Larkhill cardigan. "See?" She brings up a picture, showing the screen to Carriveau.

"Let me look at that properly." Carriveau takes the phone from her, scrutinizing a provocative lingerie shot of an attractive brunette before tapping a few buttons and handing the device back.

"What did you just do?" Rylie tries to find the picture again. "Did you delete it?" She flips all the way through her stored photos. "You did!" She puts on a serious voice. "Now you'll have to replace it."

Carriveau's answer surprises her.

"Nothing above the shoulders, or below the waist, *s'il te plaît.*"

Rylie's jaw drops. "Are you serious? You'll let me take a nudie of you?"

Carriveau shrugs. "Why not? I'm not a prude."

Leaping on the offer in case it expires, Rylie swings her leg over Carriveau, straddling her, grinding crotch against crotch. In this position, she takes a picture of Carriveau's bare breasts, her proud nipples standing to attention.

While she's saving the picture as her phone's wallpaper, completely naked, sat astride her equally naked Housemistress and teacher, an amusing thought occurs to her.

"You know, my parents decided to send me to boarding school because they thought I needed more discipline."

"Ha! That worked well, didn't it?" Carriveau reaches up and fondles Rylie's breasts. "Were your parents angry when they found out about your relationship with the German teacher?"

"Yeah, but not so much 'cause she was a teacher at my school." Rylie sets the phone aside. "Or because she was older than me, for what it's worth. There's almost twenty years between my parents, so they know that argument would never fly."

"Why, then?"

"Because she didn't have a dick."

Carriveau's ministrations falter. "*Ma chérie ...*"

"Don't worry, I'm used to it." Rylie places her hands over Carriveau's and urges her to continue. "When I was seven, I was grounded for a month after my parents caught me kissing the girl next door. She was eleven."

"After older women, even then!" Carriveau pulls her into a kiss.

As they kiss, Rylie grinds herself on Carriveau's pelvis. "Wanna go again? I'm ready."

"Ready for what?" Carriveau wants to hear her say it.

"I want to fuck you again."

Rylie tries to coax Carriveau's hand between her legs, but Carriveau rebuffs her.

"Can you say it for me *en français*?"

"*Je veux encore te baiser.*" Unsure of her syntax, Rylie raises her voice at the end of the sentence, as if posing a question.

Carriveau shakes her head. "You don't sound sure of yourself. Perhaps that's not really what you want." She continues to resist. "Try again?"

"*Fais-moi l'amour*," Rylie says instead, rubbing her piercing on Carriveau's mound, stimulating her own clit. "Make love to me."

"That's better." Carriveau rewards her with two fingers, flipping her over onto her back, eliciting a squeal and howl when she directs her fingers deep inside Rylie's cunt.

"Yes!" Rylie bucks her hips, driving Carriveau into her harder. "Fuck me!"

"*En français*," Carriveau insists. "*Parle français pour moi.*"

"*Baise-moi!*" Rylie mewls, gripping the bed sheets. "More!"

Carriveau halts. "You really want more?" She probes the young teen with long, slow strokes. "How much more?"

"I want everything." Rylie spreads her legs wider, bringing her knees up.

Dutifully, Carriveau retrieves a strapless dildo from a drawer in her bedside table.

CHAPTER SIXTEEN

FOR RYLIE, MORNING BRINGS THE SMELL OF FRESH coffee and imported French perfume. There's no screeching alarm, and no cubicle wall to accidentally bash her head on when she rolls over. The sheets are soft, the pillow cool against her cheek, and she can feel the warmth of another body behind her.

Carriveau.

Suddenly remembering where she is, she rolls onto her back, still sated from last night's passions. Her core is burning and throbbing from repeated rounds of lovemaking, her chest aching from the strain of topping Carriveau, attempting to use a strapless dildo for the first time.

As she'd feared it might, her first try resulted in three thrusts and a bout of giggles when the toy slipped out of her. She was definitely tight enough, and well in control of her pelvic muscles, but she was so wet that it was difficult to keep a grip on the end of the dildo that was lodged inside her.

"*Encore*," Carriveau encouraged her to try again, helping her to reinsert the dildo, but the second effort didn't end with much more success than the first.

After the third slip, and Rylie's escalating frustration, they'd switched positions. With a comforting kiss, Carriveau climbed on top and rode her like a circus pony, breathlessly hushing her apologies and reassuring her that it gets easier with practice.

Now, after only a few hours sleep, Rylie's ready to go for attempt number four. She flips onto her side, expecting to find a naked French goddess lying next to her, but to her great disappointment, Carriveau's already dressed for work. She's sitting on top of the covers, her legs outstretched, her back against the headboard, a laptop open on her thighs.

"*Bonjour, ma chérie.*" The French woman dips her head to smile at Rylie over her reading glasses.

"What time is it?" Rylie looks around for a clock, wondering if she overslept.

"Early." Carriveau sips from a mug of coffee, scrolling through a webpage. "You can sleep a little longer, but I have to go in for a meeting, and then I have classes until lunch."

"Another meeting?" Rylie yawns, stretching.

"With Missus Bursnell." Carriveau nurses her mug thoughtfully. "She probably wants to talk to me about Friday's concert. I can't think why else she'd want to see me." She looks down at her naked lover, grabbing a quick feel of a freely available breast. "We won't be able to do this very often, you know. Spend the whole night together."

"I've been thinking about that." Rylie shuffles into a sitting position. "I can get exeats, right? I read about them in the student handbook: permission slips to leave school premises on weekends. The book says sixth form students can get exeats to go into town and see a movie, or have dinner, or ... stay somewhere overnight."

Carriveau sets her mug aside, placing it on the bedside table, the heart-shaped picture of Kaitlyn no longer anywhere to be seen. "Are you suggesting that you use your exeats to have sex with me in the Travelodge Inn down the road?"

"It's the best thing, no? During the week, we'll have to suffer as we have been: nothing more than the occasional grope here and there. But on the weekends, we can have each other properly."

"You'll need to get permission," Carriveau warns. "Exeats are a privilege, not a right."

Rylie shrugs. "So who do I have to ask?"

"Your Housemistress."

With laughter, Rylie nestles against her. "Sorted, then." She looks down at the laptop. "Are you online? Let's book a room for next weekend." She clicks on a minimized web browser window, bringing up the last page Carriveau was looking at.

Local job listings.

Specifically, teaching positions, the field narrowed to modern languages.

Rylie stares at the screen, her heartbeat accelerating, adrenalin pumping. "You're leaving?" Her voice is whisper soft.

"I think I have to, don't you?" Carriveau strokes Rylie's hair. "Not to be away from you, but to be *with* you. As long as we both remain at this school, what we're doing is against the law." She forces Rylie to look at her. "Please don't be angry." She teases a kiss from Rylie's slightly trembling lips.

"We can make this work," Rylie pleads. "It's only for a short time, anyway. I'll be eighteen in six months, and—"

"No, Rylie," Carriveau shuts her down. "I can't keep teaching here; I can't keep teaching *you*. I don't want it to be like this. I've been down this road once before, and it didn't end well."

"You never thought about leaving when you were with Kaitlyn?"

Carriveau shakes her head. "I didn't have to: she was eighteen, and I wasn't her teacher. But still, my staying here was a mistake. I hid my feelings for her, but I won't hide my feelings for you." She closes up the laptop and pushes it to the foot of the bed, turning to face her unconvinced lover. "I'm not going to make the same mistake twice." She lays her head on Rylie's shoulder, sweeping the teen into an awkwardly positioned embrace. "I denied everything and it destroyed her." She pushes her face into Rylie's hair, kissing the side of her head. "I can't do that again."

She holds Rylie in her arms until the teen can't take it anymore.

"You're gonna collapse my lung," Rylie wheezes.

"Sorry!" Carriveau pulls back. "I didn't mean to hurt you." She cups Rylie's face. "*Je ne veux jamais te faire de mal. Tu me comprends?*"

Rylie nods, believing every word of the "I never want to hurt you," knowing well that Carriveau wouldn't consider making such a drastic change in her life unless she truly felt it was for the best.

"What am I to do today?" she asks then, getting off the subject.

"Missus Bursnell wants you to do some quiet reading in the library. I told her she can expect you there at ten o'clock promptly, after you've finished your house chores."

Rylie screws up her face. "Chores? Ugh."

"Not to worry. If she asks, tell her I had you darning loose skirt hems or something." Carriveau lays a kiss on her before sliding off the bed. "I thought you might like a lie in, since you didn't get much in the way of sleep last night."

"*Merci.*" Rylie flops back under the covers.

"I'll meet you in the library at lunchtime." Carriveau slips on her shoes. "Maybe I'll let you give me a pelvic exam in the biology aisle." Wink.

She grabs one of her silk scarves off the mirror and wraps it twice around her neck, hiding the marks of passion left behind on her milky skin, some of the bruises so severe they'll take days to heal.

Rylie's nipping and biting had been relentless, as if she were trying to devour her prey from head to toe, claiming every inch of flesh for her own possession. Over the course of the night, Carriveau's neck, shoulders, belly, and ass all became painfully acquainted with her teeth, but she'd carefully avoided any tender areas where the sensation might be unpleasurable.

190

She was hungry. From the minute they tumbled into bed together, she was ravenous for sexual contact and eager to please. She listened to Carriveau's cues and adjusted herself accordingly, never once needing to be redirected or cautioned.

Indeed, the oral sex had been far beyond anything Carriveau had ever imagined. The first time Rylie went down on her, she'd been delicate and tender, licking her and probing her with the utmost care, peppering her sensitive pink flesh with kisses. This time, she'd buried her face against Carriveau's opening, attacking her with tongue and fingers simultaneously, making her clit swell, her engorged g-spot ready to pop.

Carriveau invoked the lord's name over and over again, sometimes sandwiched in between coarse expletives—all cried out in French, of course.

Never had someone worked her cunt so vigorously, deliberately holding her on the cusp of an orgasm for so long it felt like every muscle in her body was on fire, causing her to shake uncontrollably for a good ten minutes before Rylie finally pushed her over the edge.

And when it finally came, the climax Rylie gave her was the strongest she'd ever felt. She gushed all over the bed sheets, drenching the young teen's face, her entire body racked with convulsions, and she howled at the top of her lungs, wailing so loudly that she probably woke up students in the neighboring house.

That was round one.

More followed.

After lapping her up and giving her a brief respite, Rylie tongued her clit again, bringing her to another peak that was more subdued than the first, but no less exquisite.

Then Carriveau took over.

Unable to go even one more second without tasting the beautiful young woman lying beside her, she spread Rylie's legs and dived in between, groaning with delight at the unbelievable sweetness that greeted her tongue. Rylie was dripping with arousal, the valley between her labia so flushed and wet, her opening slick enough to allow three fingers to push slowly inside her, but so tight that Carriveau's slender digits were wedged in her hot sex, barely able to move.

Experimenting with different sensations, she withdrew to one finger and moved it in fast circles while tonguing her clit, then added a second finger and began tapping that special button of skin inside her, causing her to pant and grip fistfuls of the sheets. Her orgasm was less volcanic than Carriveau's, but resulted in just as much noise.

Wiping the cat-that-got-the-cream smile off her face before entering the main school building, Carriveau checks her appearance in the 'Are you presentable?' mirror, making sure none of Rylie's exuberance is showing before heading toward Missus Bursnell's office. Along the way, she passes three of her peers.

While she smiles and greets them in passing, they flash her wary looks, their conversations dropping to low whispers. Their reactions are so abnormal that, by the time she knocks on the door to the Headmistress's office, she has the distinct impression that she's about to be punished for something very, very bad.

"Please, Vivienne, have a seat," Missus Bursnell commands from behind her sturdy oak desk, not a single wisp of her tightly-bunned gray hair out of place. "Have you checked your school e-mails this morning?"

Carriveau's never known her to be quite this abrupt. Usually a fan of pointless small talk, she often has to be prompted to get to the point of her conversations. But not today.

In answer to the question, Carriveau shakes her head. "I normally do that in my office before my first class. *Pourquoi?*" She reminds herself to speak English. "Why?"

"It seems an e-mail intended for you was accidentally sent out to the entire faculty." She hands a sheet of paper across the desk. "Damn that pesky 'send all' button."

Having no clue what she could've done to incur such hostility, Carriveau begins reading the e-mail with a look of mild annoyance ... but that soon fades.

Purportedly from Rylie, the e-mail peppers proclamations of love with increasingly graphic details of their few sexual encounters. Namely, their midnight fuck in the Lower Sixth dormitory, and their brief but tender lovemaking in Carriveau's private quarters on Sunday night.

Carriveau's chest tightens as she reaches the end of the note, her hands shaking. Could Rylie be this stupid? Could she be this careless? Why would she write it in English? Surely she'd make the effort to pen something this intimate in French. Of course she would. And she'd write it on a piece of notepaper and stick it in a bowl of Skittles. She'd never ... ever ...

The timestamp on the e-mail settles it: it was sent at eleven o'clock last night. At that time, Carriveau was two fingers deep in her, building her up to her third orgasm.

"What is this?" Carriveau tosses the paper back onto Missus Bursnell's desk. "Rylie Harcourt didn't write it."

"It was sent from her student account," the Headmistress counters.

"I don't care." Carriveau clenches her jaw. "Rylie *didn't* send this."

"How can you be so sure?"

For a split second, Carriveau considers telling a lie. Then, she remembers all that she said to Rylie in bed, and all the promises she'd made.

No denial.

No weakness.

Fuck Larkhill.

Fuck priggish Missus Bursnell.

The fear ebbs away and Carriveau relaxes, the tension in her posture dissipating. "Because she was with me when this was sent."

Missus Bursnell fails to grasp the significance of that. "She was with you after lights out?" The perpetual lines on her brow deepen. "Why?"

"Because we were in bed together." Carriveau locks eyes with her. "Having sex."

Silence.

Missus Bursnell's face turns an interesting shade of purple.

"Sorry," Carriveau volunteers scathingly. "Was that not the answer you wanted?"

"How could you do this again?" The ascetic Headmistress crunches the printed e-mail in her fist. "I've tolerated your"—she searches for an inoffensive word—"sexual liberation thus far because you're an exceptional teacher, and your parents are longstanding benefactors of this institution, but—"

"Sexual liberation?" Carriveau cuts in. "Are you referring to my being gay? Or my perfectly legal relationship with an eighteen-year-old woman that you deemed inappropriate merely because it bothered your delicate sensibilities?"

"This is scandalous!" Missus Bursnell brings her fist down upon her desk. "The Harcourt child is *not* eighteen!"

"Would it make a difference to you if she was?" Carriveau confronts the Headmistress's prejudice directly. "The woman I loved killed herself because you couldn't bear the thought of two women making love under your roof. You told the entire school that her feelings for me were a dangerous, childish infatuation. You insinuated that she was mentally ill and ought to seek psychiatric help."

"The girl stood on top of a dining table in the refectory and swore her love for you. That behavior is not normal, Miss Carriveau."

"She was defending herself!" Carriveau snaps. "She was being bullied, as I had mentioned to you some

194

weeks before. Someone was sending her anonymous threats and taunts, calling her a whore and a slut, insinuating that she was prostituting herself to me. I asked you to help me get to the bottom of it, but you chose to ignore me." Carriveau almost brings herself to tears. "She couldn't take any more. She declared her love for me, and you called her damaged."

Carriveau pauses to collect herself, determined to reach the end of her tirade without falling apart. "Do you know what the worst part of it is?" She sniffs. "You did all this, and I let you. I kept my mouth shut. I denied loving her because you convinced me that silence was the best policy, and that I had a professional loyalty and duty to my employer that came paramount to my romantic feelings."

"It would've ended your career!"

"It ended her life!" A tear spills from Carriveau's damp eyes, her hands trembling again, this time with anger. "Don't you care at all?"

"I did what had to be done."

"For whose benefit?" Carriveau digs a tissue out of her pocket and dabs at her eyes. "Not Kaitlyn's. Not mine. Only your own."

"For the benefit of the school," Missus Bursnell barks indignantly, as if that in any way mitigates the loss of a life and the denigration that followed it.

"No. It was for *your* benefit," Carriveau snarls. "For the *reputation* of the school, which you couldn't bear to see sullied by the public acknowledgement of a romantic entanglement between two women." More tears of anger fall. "You disgust me."

"The feeling is perfectly mutual." Missus Bursnell glowers at her. "And I've a good mind to call the police."

"The police?!" Carriveau laughs.

"You spent the night with a student!"

"I did, and if you call the police, everyone will know about it. What do you think that would do for the reputation of your precious school?"

Missus Bursnell grits her teeth. "I think it's time our professional association with one another was terminated. Don't you, Vivienne?"

"*Docteure Carriveau, s'il vous plaît, Madame.*" Carriveau dries her eyes, her burden lifted. "And I quite agree: I quit." She says that with a smile. "Now might I politely suggest that you put your prejudices aside and find the girl responsible for sending this e-mail. You may very well prevent another tragedy from occurring on your campus by punishing her accordingly, instead of brushing it under the carpet because the subject matter isn't to your taste."

Missus Bursnell swivels her green leather chair and consults her computer screen. "It was sent from a terminal in your house."

"*Non, c'est impossible.*" Carriveau reverts to her first tongue accidentally. "That's impossible. Rylie Harcourt is the only girl left in my house."

"Not according to my register." Missus Bursnell clicks buttons infuriatingly slowly.

Carriveau's blood turns to ice. "What? Who?"

"One other girl." Missus Bursnell turns the screen to face her. "Adel Edwards."

Carriveau shakes her head, disbelieving. "No ... she went on the trip with the others."

"The coach sign-in chart says otherwise." Missus Bursnell checks the e-mailed file on her phone. "She never boarded."

"So she never left seclusion?"

"Seclusion?" Missus Bursnell frowns.

"I sent her to seclusion the night before last." Carriveau tightens her fist around the wadded up tissue, irritation seeping through her. "She was misbehaving quite terribly."

"You *sent* her there?" Missus Bursnell clarifies. "Or you *took* her there?"

Carriveau drops her head into her hands. "I sent her there," she replies meekly.

"So if she wasn't in seclusion, and she didn't go on the trip ..." Missus Bursnell leans on her desk, demanding answers. "Where was she last night? And where is she now?"

Carriveau reaches a thoroughly horrifying conclusion. "She's in my house." And that leads to an even more horrifying fear. "Rylie!"

CHAPTER SEVENTEEN

BAREFOOT, CLAD IN HER COTTON NIGHTDRESS, Rylie sings to herself in the kitchen, making a quick piece of toast before going back to bed to laze in Carriveau's sex-stained sheets for as long as possible before having to get up and head to the library.

She doesn't bother to use a plate, and trails crumbs from the kitchen to the staircase, munching down the last bite before she hits the first step. Her body still flooded with endorphins, she skips up the stairs, singing softly all the while. She makes for the Lower Sixth dormitory to fetch her MP3 player, but stops short of the door, cutting off her singing mid-song.

When she got out of bed to grab some breakfast, she left the door to Carriveau's rooms open so that she wouldn't lock herself out, and now the unmistakable sound of running water is emanating from within.

"Vivienne?" she calls out, stepping closer. "Are you back already?"

No response.

"Vivienne?" She peeks her head inside and tiptoes to the bathroom, finding the tub dangerously full, steam rising from it. "Shit!" She turns off the taps. "Vivienne, where are you?"

Sensing movement in her periphery, she spins to face her lover, only to have the world cast into complete darkness. She barely registers the impact of the laptop against the side of her head, nor the slap of the cold tiles against her falling body.

She's out cold.

Then, she feels a prick. Like a needle piercing her skin, it reminds her of an allergy test she once had. She was just a kid, but she remembers the sensation of a dozen needles being jabbed into her inner forearm, a few inches above her wrist.

Her wrist.

The sharp pain is centered there, and it brings some lucidity back. She's wet. Very wet, and all over, her skin tingling from the heat.

She's in the bathtub.

She opens her eyes, but her vision's blurred. There's a figure leaning over the tub, something glinting in the bright bathroom lights. Blinking several times, squinting against the glare, more detail comes to the shadowy mass above her.

Mousy brown hair.

A Larkhill uniform.

It's Adel! And that shimmering thing in her hand ... a razorblade!

"What the fuck?!" Rylie yanks back her hand as Adel drives the blade downward.

Blood surges from the wound. Dark rivulets run down her arm and into the tub, turning the water crimson, and her vision blurs again. The sight of blood has always made her woozy.

Summoning every bit of her strength, she pushes her hips up and uses her powerful legs to kick Adel away from the bathtub, sending her attacker flying backwards, the razorblade scuttering across the floor.

Adel falls on her backside, jarring her tailbone, momentarily disorienting her.

"I was right about you!" Rylie growls. "You're mental!"

She tries to pull herself out of the bath, but she can't bear her own weight, her sliced wrist impeding her efforts, even though she's not cut as deeply as Adel had intended.

"All you had to do was keep your hands off Vivienne." Adel gets on her knees, looking around for the lost blade. "I tried warning you," she grumbles, "but you wouldn't listen."

Rylie anchors herself to the edge of the tub, holding her head above the water. "It won't work, you know." She curls her fingers around the cool porcelain, now slick with blood. "You think you'll just be able to swoop in and take advantage of Vivienne, like you did when Kaitlyn died, but that's not going to happen. She doesn't want you. She'll never want you."

"That's what Kaitlyn said." Adel abandons her search for the razorblade and looms over the tub again. "Right before her neck snapped."

Rylie clings to the slippery ceramic, numb and woozy, her fuzzy brain scarcely able to make the connection. "You killed her?" she rasps, her vision graying. "You killed Kaitlyn!"

"I had to," Adel contends, easing Rylie away from the side of the bath with a sickening degree of coolness, as if this is little more than a chore. "She wouldn't leave Vivienne alone either."

Rylie sinks back into the warm water. She feels Adel's hand on her forehead, forcing her under, but she's incapable of exerting any resistance. She struggles and flails her limbs, clutching handfuls of empty air, reaching out for help. She holds her breath for as long as she can, but her lungs were almost empty when she was dunked, so only a few seconds pass before ...

The pressure's lifted.

Her ears submerged, she can hear dull thuds outside the tub.

Adel's head hitting the ceramic sink.

Her unconscious body hitting the floor.

A moment later, Rylie feels something grasping at her chest.

She gasps, her torso pulled up from the water by her nightdress, her neck cradled in a small, gentle hand. In one swift motion, her upper body is flung over the side of the bath, her head down, and she's able to cough a small amount of inhaled water out of her lungs.

"Rylie!" A familiar voice calls her name, tapping her cheeks.

It's Carriveau.

She helps Rylie out of the tub and sits with her on the floor, wrapping a towel around her shoulders, moving wet hair away from her face, ensuring that she can breathe unobstructed.

Blood is pouring over her nightdress, over her thighs, and pooling on the floor.

So much blood.

"Oh, darling!" Carriveau tugs the silk scarf off her neck and ties it around Rylie's wrist, somewhat stemming the flow of blood. "The police are on their way. An ambulance, too." She pulls Rylie to her chest, raising the gashed wrist up above the level of Rylie's heart.

"How did you know?" Rylie croaks, sinking into Carriveau's breast.

"Edwards sent an e-mail from your student account to every teacher at Larkhill, revealing intimate and explicit details of our ..." Carriveau scrolls through a mental list of choices.

Affair.

Fling.

Indiscretions.

"... Relationship." She holds Rylie in her arms, kissing and squeezing her. "When I realized she hadn't left on the sixth form trip, I was afraid she might try to hurt you again."

"She needs help," Rylie murmurs hoarsely. "She's a fucking nutcase."

"*Je sais.*" Carriveau cries into Rylie's wet hair, translating herself out of habit. "I know."

"No, you don't." Rylie coughs, finding it difficult to breathe, her chest in chronic pain. "Kaitlyn didn't kill herself—it was Adel."

"What?" Carriveau's tears stem, her concern for Rylie momentarily overridden by the recurring pain of this old, festering wound.

"Kaitlyn's death wasn't your fault," Rylie asserts with conviction. "Adel got rid of her because she wanted you for herself." Her breaths grow shallower by the second, her body limper and limper. "You didn't do anything wrong."

Carriveau breaks down, the release of her guilt dwarfed by the fear of losing another lover.

"I love you, Rylie." She tries to hold up the teen's head. "I love you so much."

"I know." Rylie smiles, blacking out in her arms.

EPILOGUE

Several weeks later ...

CARRIVEAU PULLS UP OUTSIDE A LARGE, RED BRICK country house in Kent, her tires crunching on the gravel driveway. A gardener waves politely to her and carries about his business, tending to the flowerbeds on either side of an ornate front door that's framed by even more ornate marble pillars.

Taking a steadying breath, she glances down at the passenger seat and scoops up a fresh bouquet of purple orchids and white lilies, then steps out of the car.

Her long hair is unrestrained, bouncing over her shoulders, framing her face. Her tight black dress is slightly creased from the drive, but there's nothing she can do about that now. Walking carefully over the gravel in her black patent stilettos, she approaches the front door and rings the bell, hoping her nerves aren't too apparent.

Missus Harcourt—a surprisingly young blonde woman, yet to hit forty—answers, wearing pearls and a floral print garden dress.

"*Bonjour, Madame.*" Carriveau beams. "My name is Vivienne Carriveau. If you remember, we met briefly at the hospital after ... well, some weeks ago. I was your daughter's Housemistress at Larkhill."

Missus Harcourt nods, casting her eyes over the French woman on her doorstep, her expression sour. "I know who you are."

"These are for you." Carriveau presents her with the flowers. "May I come in?"

"I suppose you're here to talk about what happened? Now that it's all over with." The standoffish woman accepts the flowers and leads Carriveau into the front room, offering her a seat on an antique chaise. "I appreciate you coming all this way, but there was really no need."

"*Madame*?" Carriveau questions her, looking around the room.

Everything is floral: the wallpaper, the furniture coverings, the rugs, and the lampshades. An older man, whom Carriveau recognizes as Mister Harcourt, is standing beside the fireplace, smoking a cigar, dressed in something he would probably describe as casual attire: trousers and a dress shirt, sans tie.

"We're not going to take any action against the school," Missus Harcourt explains, as if money could be the only logical reason for Carriveau's visit.

"Oh, I—" Carriveau doesn't get any further.

"You again," Mister Harcourt mumbles, looking Carriveau over in much the same way as his wife had done, but with an added pinch of suspicion. "Why did Larkhill send you? We already agreed not to go to the press about this rotten business."

"Actually, I'm no longer employed at Larkhill," Carriveau sets them straight. "I've recently taken up a position at Grange Road Secondary School. That's where Rylie studied for her GCSEs, no? I'm their new Head of Modern Languages."

"Your point?" Missus Harcourt sighs.

"I wasn't sent here," Carriveau explains. "I came of my own accord." She hesitates to add more. "The nature of my visit is ... personal."

A brief silence hugs the air.

Missus Harcourt clicks her jaw. "Hmm, well, what can I say? If you're worried about the news of your sordid behavior with our daughter being made public, then you may sleep easier knowing that your reckless indiscretion is as much an embarrassment to us as I'm certain it must be to you."

"With respect"—Carriveau remains outwardly calm, her nerves racked—"I'm not embarrassed about my conduct with your daughter. I fell in love with her, and for that, I feel no regret."

"She was your student!" Missus Harcourt gears up for a verbal assault. "You're lucky that awful child who attacked Rylie and took that other poor girl's life is stark raving mad and no-one believed a word she said against you. Now she's locked up in a loony bin and you're here, in my house. Why? If not to apologize for taking advantage of a seventeen-year-old girl."

Lost for words, Carriveau flaps her jaw, no sound escaping. Fortunately, she's saved by the sound of socked feet rushing down a carpeted staircase.

Thunk, thunk, thunk, thunk, thunk ...

Rylie appears in the doorway.

She's wearing stonewash jeans, a white shirt, and a black waistcoat. Her hair's down—and brushed, for once—her wrists adorned with leather wristbands, charity bracelets, and of course, her rainbow beads.

"Hi." She grins at Carriveau.

"*Bonjour,*" Carriveau stands, patting the folds out of her dress.

Still grinning, Rylie dashes to her and pulls her into an embrace. "I've missed you so much."

She buries her face in Carriveau's hair, breathing her in deep, marinating in the comfortingly familiar scent of her perfume. Then, she pulls back to admire her outfit, holding her firmly by the hips.

"I feel underdressed."

"Nonsense." Carriveau fingers her long blonde locks. "You look perfect."

"Perfect for what?" Mister Harcourt asks, killing the last of his cigar in an ashtray.

"We're going out to dinner," Rylie exclaims proudly, taking Carriveau by the hand, an angry red scar on her wrist peeking out from her shirt cuff.

"You most certainly are not!" Rylie's mother gets to her feet, ready to physically restrain her child if necessary. "This woman is—"

"My girlfriend," Rylie cuts her off. "This woman is my girlfriend, mum."

"But she's—"

"Amazing," Rylie shoves words in her mother's mouth. "And I love her, and I'm not giving her up for anything." She tugs Carriveau toward the door. "Come on, let's go."

"Wait." Rylie's father stops them in the entrance hall while Rylie zips on a pair of ankle boots, his eyes flitting down to the entwined fingers of his daughter and her former teacher. "How do you think Grange Road Secondary would feel about this?" Carriveau is the focus of his words. "One of their teachers taking a sixth former out to dinner."

"I shouldn't think they'd have a great deal to say on the matter, since Rylie isn't a student of theirs," Carriveau answers boldly. "She attends the neighboring Grange Road Sixth Form College, which is an entirely separate educational institution."

"We're not doing anything wrong, dad." Rylie sighs, grabbing her house keys. "So just let it go, yeah? I'll see you later." She rethinks that. "Maybe tomorrow, if my date goes well! But don't worry, I promise I won't let Vivienne get me pregnant."

In fits of laughter, she pulls Carriveau out of the house and helps her across the gravel driveway back to the car, then pushes her up against it and lays a deep kiss on her.

"So you still want me?" Carriveau captures her lips again. "Even though I'm no longer your teacher? Or your Housemistress?"

"*J'ai envie de toi, Vivienne.*" Rylie holds her close. "*J'ai envie de toi.*"

THE END

ABOUT THE AUTHOR

 Keira Michelle Telford is an award-winning author with a love for the gruesome, the macabre, and the downright filthy. She writes dystopian science fiction, erotic lesbian romance, and other lesbian fiction.

Website: www.keiramichelle.com
Facebook: www.facebook.com/keiramichelletelford
Goodreads: www.goodreads.com/keiramichelle
Amazon: www.amazon.com/author/keiramichelle

Series by this author:

The SILVER Series
www.ellacross.com

The Prisonworld Trilogy
www.carmenwild.com

Standalone titles:

Cadence of My Heart – an erotic lesbian romance
The Ruin of Us – a Victorian erotic lesbian romance
Quicunque Vult – a gritty Victorian romance
Hoar & Rime (A Short Story) – lesbian fiction
Evonnia & the Maiden (A Short Story) – erotic lesbian fiction
Falling Hard (A Novelette) – lesbian fiction

18786930R00118

Printed in Great Britain
by Amazon